P9-DNF-056

When Elves
ATTACK

TIM DORSEY

When Elves
ATTACK

A Joyous Christmas Greeting from the

Criminal Nutbars of the Sunshine State

WILLIAM MORROW

An Imprint of HarperCollins*Publishers*

HarperCollins books may be purchased for educational, business, or sales promotional use. For information please write: Special Markets Department, HarperCollins Publishers, 10 East 53rd Street, New York, NY 10022.

Design by John D. Lewis

Library of Congress Cataloging-in-Publication Data has been applied for.

ISBN 978-0-06-209284-7

11 12 13 14 15   OV/RRD   10 9 8 7 6 5 4 3 2

For Henry Ferris

I stopped believing in Santa Claus when my mother took me to see him in a department store, and he asked for my autograph.

—SHIRLEY TEMPLE

When Elves
ATTACK

PROLOGUE

My name is Edith Grabowski. I'm ninety-three years old, and I've decided to stop having sex.

I guess you just reach a certain age.

There are only so many positions. Even fewer with the medical equipment. And the scares are more and more frequent. The guy shows up and smiles, "I brought my little blue pills," like it's the funniest romantic line ever. An hour later, his eyes bug out. "My heart! My heart!" And just before we hit the Life Alert button, "No, wait, another false alarm. Where were we?" Then he thinks we just simply pick up where we left off. You get old enough, you realize that's the difference between men and women. Stopping to grab the nitroglycerin tablets is a definite mood-kill.

Oh, and venereal disease. All these TV stations now reporting that some of the highest rates of STD in Florida are at senior citizen communities.

That's true, look it up on the Internet.

It's usually those places that have clubhouses and aqua-therapy swimming pools and newsletters with calendars of things to do. And I'm here to tell you they ain't listing everything.

So anyway, here we are backstage. Me and my girlfriends. *Again.* Another round of the TV shows. I mean what are the odds? It's the third time in our lives we've landed in the middle of a major news event.

Make that four. But the first time doesn't really count. It was more of a feel-good story. Fifteen years ago, me and the girls started a little investment club during our morning coffee klatch. Something to do while knitting. And we blew away like ninety percent of the mutual fund managers. What's the big deal? We just read those glossy financial magazines with profiles of CEOs and picked companies run by the hottest hunks. But then the media got ahold of it and went bonkers, like us old people can do nothing but sit around playing pinochle and pooping our pants. There are three of us besides me: Eunice, Edna, and Ethel. So they dubbed us the E-Team, without even asking. We said bullshit on that alliteration. We all have grandchildren, and renamed ourselves the G-Unit. It's what they have to call us. It's in the contracts.

But back to today's story. That's why we're at the TV studio. It's a Christmas tale. Except not one you've remotely heard before. Like the other times we were in the news, it all swirled around our neighbors, the Davenports. Mainly Jim Davenport. And he's such a mild-mannered person you can't help but feel sorry for him. I don't see how he holds up.

In just over a decade, three weird blowups of violence and mayhem. Again, what are the odds?

Here are the odds:

Serge.

He started hanging around Jim again during the holidays. They say Serge is a serial killer. I didn't get that vibe. He's just another Florida lunatic, hyperactive as they come. He has this sort of offbeat charm, and not too hard on the eyes if you ask me. I said I'd given up sex, but I'd let him eat crackers in my bed.

So now we're back on the TV circuit. And even though it's a great story with enough action for three movies, the TV people still just want to ask about our sex lives, especially the VD angle at the senior centers. They have such a knee-slapping good time bringing it up and joking about those commercials for "Active Retirement Communities." Last time they asked, I turned to Eunice: "Tell 'em how you gave us all the crabs from the sofa where we play pinochle." Talk about your screeching halt. The show's anchor acted like his head had just burst into flames, and they cut to a commercial. They don't ask those questions anymore.

Hold it, the TV people just gave us the signal. We're on in five minutes.

All the stations have these spunky hostesses. Supposed to tend to our needs backstage, patronizing us because of our age. Smiling and using a singsong voice like you'd talk to a toddler: Would we like juice and cookies? No, vodka. They're mostly blondes with fake boobs. Sluts.

So here's what we do: When the hostess says we're at

the two-minute mark, one of us gets a funny look, stands up, and turns around. "I just pooped myself. Hurry up and wipe me before we go on. We only have two minutes!"

The woman usually turns white and runs off.

And then me and the girls giggle our fucking dentures loose.

Here we go. One minute to airtime. The hostess just ran off. We can hear the audience applauding.

Story time again. It all started just over a month ago, right before Thanksgiving . . .

CHAPTER ONE

A bulbous head popped up from the backseat of a 1972 Chevelle. Bloodshot eyes. Hair staging a riot.

"What time is it?"

"Right before Thanksgiving," said the driver.

"I mean time of day."

"When you usually get up. Sunset."

"Oooo, don't feel good." A hair-of-the-dog flask went to the passenger's lips. The Chevelle raced east across the Gandy Bridge.

A hand went up in the backseat. "Serge?"

Serge looked in his rearview. "Yes, you in the rear. Coleman has a question?"

"Where are we?"

The Chevelle came off the bridge with a bounce, and Serge pointed a digital camera out the driver's window. *Click, click click* . . . "See that welcome sign?"

"Yeah?"

"Any clues?"

Coleman shook his head.

" 'Welcome to Tampa' generally means we're not somewhere else."

"We're back in Tampa?"

"I'd like to see a flashier sign, though. Something with lightning bolts, titty bars, and sandwiches."

"Are you off your meds again?"

"Yes." Serge chugged a thermos of coffee. "This place has some of the best Cuban sandwiches in the country. We need a slogan, too. And not the old slogan. Know what the old slogan was? I'll tell you!" Serge tossed the thermos over his shoulder.

"Ow." Coleman rubbed his forehead.

"The old slogan was this: 'Tampa: America's Next Great City.' I've heard of playing the politics of low expectations, but what the hell?"

"It's not a good slogan?"

Serge made a skidding right on Westshore Boulevard. "Coleman, the slogan is so bad that the human brain wasn't designed to process it. Or at least its journey: A college president actually presented someone with a marketing diploma, and then later someone else handed that same person a bunch of money for those words. Was everyone drunk at that slogan meeting? I mean, what the fuck were they rejecting? 'Tampa: Still waiting for the Milwaukee-Racine hub to blow the bond rating,' or 'Visit again soon: Almost got our shit together.' "

"I like the last one." Coleman began climbing over into the front seat.

"At least it's truth in advertising—" Serge quickly raised his right arm. "Watch the foot!"

"Whoa! Need a little help here."

"I'm driving."

A brief flurry of flailing.

"It's okay now. I'm good."

Serge looked over to the passenger side. "Coleman, your head's down at the floorboards again and your legs are on the seat."

"I know. It's weird." He twisted the end of a joint in his mouth and flicked a Bic. "At least the cops can't see me burning a number this way."

"It's baffling that more people don't ride like that."

Coleman exhaled a pot cloud up toward his feet. "Tell me about it."

Another skidding turn. Serge raised his hand again to block Coleman's legs.

"Serge?"

"We have another question from the marijuana section. Proceed."

"Why do you have that gun?"

"What gun?" Serge looked toward his left hand, where he was steering with a 9mm Glock pistol for all traffic to see. "Oh, this thing?" He waved the weapon around the Chevelle's interior. "Completely forgot I was holding this." Serge aimed the gun out the window and squinted with one eye closed. Then made a shooting sound with his mouth.

"But why *are* you holding it?" asked Coleman.

"Getting ready for the holidays." Serge racked the slide,

chambering a fresh round. "You know how I love this time of year."

"Anyone particular in mind for that thing?"

"Actually yes. Thanks for reminding me." He flipped open a cell phone and hit speed dial. "Manny? Serge here . . ."

Coleman exhaled another Cheech hit. "You mean from Manny's Towing and Salvage?"

"Pipe down, chowderhead! Can't you see I'm busy with a steering wheel, cell phone, and gun? Don't be irresponsible and distract me— . . . No, not you Manny. Drugs are involved. Long story, explain later. Listen, anything further on That Thing? . . . I see, I understand . . . You're keeping your ears open, and I'll be the first person you call . . . Peace, out." Serge clapped the phone shut and aimed the gun from the window again.

Bang.

"Shit! How'd that go off?" Serge hit the gas. "We have to get the hell out of here." Rubber squealed. "And stop smoking that dope. You'll draw attention . . ."

D id you hear a gunshot?" asked Martha Davenport.

Jim Davenport looked around from the driver's seat of a white Hyundai. "Where?"

"Watch out!"

Jim cut the wheel at the last second, rubbing tires on a curb.

A '72 Chevelle whipped past them within inches and accelerated.

Jim let his car come to a stop, waiting for his heart to calm down.

"Why are you stopping?" asked Martha.

Rapid breaths. "Just collecting myself. That was close."

"But they're getting away!" Martha pointed out the windshield. "I want their license number!"

Jim sighed and sat. "Martha, you can't keep reporting everybody."

"Jim, what's wrong with you?" asked his wife. "That Charger almost hit us!"

"I think it was a Chevelle."

"Do you always have to disagree with me?"

"No—"

"That's disagreeing."

"Yes?"

"Then stop it."

"Okay."

He put the car back in gear and proceeded under the speed limit. "I know why you're upset."

Martha stared out her window. "I hate this time of year."

"But it's the holidays."

"It's a nightmare," said Martha. "Like I don't have enough to do: cook the turkey dinner, get the artificial tree down from the attic, shop at those madhouse malls, put the lights up outside, address Christmas cards to people we never see anymore because they still send us cards and we *might* see them again . . . It's too much pressure."

"That's not the real reason," said Jim.

"What is the reason?"

"My mom."

"Why do we have to let her visit anyway?"

"Because she's my mom."

Martha folded her arms tight. "Whenever it's this time of year, and the days grow closer to holiday dinners with her, I'm not even thinking about it, but the stress just subconsciously builds."

"Because you let it." Jim changed lanes and pulled into a grocery-store parking lot. "Relax and let me handle her."

"That's easy for you to say." Martha grabbed her purse off the seat. "You're not the one under the microscope. You're her son. You can do no wrong. But she watches me like a hawk, every move I make, everything I say, every dish I cook . . ."

"You're imagining things."

"Whenever I offer her iced tea or something, she rewashes the glass. And it's right out of the cabinet, like I don't keep a clean house."

"She's probably not even aware she's doing it."

"Oh, she knows all right. You're just blind to the whole mother-in-law-versus-daughter thing. It's all-out war. I think she's actually making lists and studying her battle plan for hours, because it's always the same pattern. First she fluffs the couch cushions, then wipes down the bathroom sinks, then asks if I have bleach. *Bleach!* Men don't care, but between women, bleach is a laser-guided bomb. Everything she does means something. Like when she asks you to say grace before dinner."

"What's wrong with that?"

"It's an attack on me. She knows you converted when we got married, but that's her way of pretending we never told her. She's passive-aggressive like that. Not to mention her supposedly idle comments."

"Maybe they really are idle."

"Jim! Every visit without fail, right in the middle of when I finally think everything's going nice for once, she stops and turns: 'I'll be dead soon.'"

"But your mom says the same thing."

Martha shook her head. "Another holiday war."

"But she's your mom."

"She thinks your perfect, too," said Martha. "Concerned I'm not feeding you properly. And it's been too long since I visited my cousin."

"The one who got out of prison?"

"Plus she keeps hinting about moving in with us." She stared out the window again. "I'd have to kill myself."

Jim drove down a row of cars near the front of the store. "There's a spot."

Martha pulled a purse strap over her shoulder. "Let's just go get the turkey."

"I'll get the bleach."

"Not funny."

"Only trying to lighten the mood."

"Watch out!"

Jim cut the wheel, almost clipping four parked cars. A Delta 88 whipped by on the left and screeched around the corner.

"Jim! Go after him!" She pulled out a notepad and pen. "I only got the first three numbers."

Jim parked instead and turned with understanding eyes.

"Oh, so take his side."

"Martha, maybe it's a dangerous person. Just like the Chevelle. He's already demonstrated a reckless lifestyle. That's a red flag."

"And that's why the authorities need to know. Start the car! He's getting away!"

"You can't stop every jerk in the city."

"But if everyone else did their part."

"Look, you're right, he's a menace. But now he's driven out of our lives. The last thing we need to do is reel him back in. And we know nothing about him. He could be capable of anything for revenge."

"You're paranoid."

"Martha, my job involves threat assessment. The odds are slim, but if we report enough people . . ."

"You and your red flags."

"I love you."

She opened her door. "I hate this time of year."

A black Delta 88 came flying around the corner on MacDill Avenue. The driver wanted to make the traffic light, but it was a short yellow, and the sedan screeched to a stop just after it turned red.

A convertible Mustang pulled up alongside. Four frat

boys with baseball caps on backward. The horn honked. One of the frat boys made a cranking motion with his hand for the driver of the Delta 88 to roll down his window.

The glass slowly lowered.

"Hey, asshole!" yelled the Mustang's driver. "You almost hit us back there. Are you retarded or something?"

The door of the Delta 88 opened. A man in a uniform got out and approached the sports car. "I'm really sorry. My mother's in the hospital and my mind's been elsewhere—"

Suddenly the man nailed the Mustang's driver in the jaw with a wicked sucker punch. Then he reached in and playfully pinched the driver's cheek. "Advice for the day: Don't fuck with people you know nothing about. I see you again, I'll kill you."

The man got back in the Delta 88 and sped off.

The Mustang remained stopped at the green light. Four shocked faces. One was crying.

W atch out!" yelled Coleman, grabbing the dashboard.

Serge cut the wheel. A Delta 88 screamed by. "Typical Tampa driver."

Coleman relit his dropped joint. "Someone should report him."

The Chevelle continued south on Dale Mabry Highway.

"I love this time of year," said Serge, ejecting a bullet from his Glock and stowing it under the seat for safety.

"Every time the weather turns cool in Florida, it subconsciously triggers déjà vu memories of past holiday seasons."

Coleman cracked a beer. "Like what?"

"Getting cool toys for Christmas. Even better, getting shit I didn't like and blowing it up with firecrackers. My folks were always puzzled by the debris."

"I blew up something I made of LEGOs."

"That's the primary use of LEGOs, even though they keep quiet about it." Serge put his fingers together, assembling something invisible. "The interlocking blocks allowed flexibility of design so you can engineer a directional charge. Excellent demolition training, which was otherwise unavailable at that age."

Coleman killed the beer and crunched the can flat against his forehead. "Ow, I think I cut myself . . . Any other memories?"

"There's also the newer ones." Serge handed him some napkins. "Like every year, newspapers run the exact same menu of holiday stories: family hospitalized for smoke inhalation trying to keep warm by barbecuing indoors, seven crushed in Black Friday shopping spree, needy family evicted from apartment just days before Christmas, moms arrested fighting over last Xbox, employees laid off just days before Christmas, car stolen from shopping center with all of family's gifts in trunk, man dies watering Christmas tree with lights on, depression soars during holidays, evicted needy family gets holiday wish, hospitals warn about eating Christmas decorations that aren't food, needy family's hoax results in charges. It's a special time of year."

"Are we there yet?" asked Coleman.

"Just up ahead. I checked us into our new room before dawn while you were still unconscious at the old one."

Coleman glanced at their surroundings, detecting a trend. Sports bars, Tex-Mex, bowling alleys. Strip malls offering tattoos, guns, and haircuts. Off-brand convenience stores with large ads for lottery tickets, Newport cigarettes, and Asian groceries. An unnatural concentration of personal-injury-attorney signs at bus stops. Gas stations selling fried poultry and hash pipes. The pimp-your-ride industry: auto-detailing, auto upholstery, window tinting, auto alarm. Grime-streaked apartment balconies full of dead potted plants, barbecues, and people banging on doors. Old mom-and-pop motel signs with patriotic motifs involving eagles, flags, military airplanes, and primitive rocket ships. And finally the sub-budget motels with no signs at all.

Coleman took another hit. "Where are we?"

"South Tampa." Serge hit his blinker. "More specifically south of Gandy Boulevard, toward the air-force base. The closer you get to the base, the sketchier the highway. Here we are, a sub-budget motel with no sign, which is perfect." He turned the wheel.

"Perfect?"

"The behavior of the guests at these motels is so erratic that our mission will go unnoticed."

"What's our mission?"

Serge pulled into a parking lot. "The story on the news a few days ago about the VFW hall. Not one of the holiday stories I mentioned, but since it's during the season, it's that much more despicable."

Coleman opened his passenger door and tumbled onto

the pavement. He popped back up. "Something tripped me again . . . What happened at the VFW?"

"The economy. There's been a huge increase in desperate, low-end burglars ripping off heavy metal stuff right in the open and selling it for scrap." Serge got out a key and headed for their room. "Chain-link fence, sheds, aluminum siding. One guy up in Pasco even used a cutting torch and took a span of guardrail from the expressway."

"But we've done that. Remember our U-Haul full of metal garbage cans and spools of barbed wire?"

"I'm not saying it's wrong. In fact it creates jobs far more aggressively than any stimulus package. I'd love to see a Discovery Channel special tracking the illegal hauls to the scrap yard, where it's crushed, loaded on tractor trailers, driven to Pittsburgh, infusing capital into local diners, bars, and truck-stop hookers, finally reaching the foundry, where it's smelted, shipped again to assembly lines in Terra Haute and Fond du Lac, which use the raw materials to manufacture new stuff to replace the shit we stole, then sending it back to Florida, creating more employment for contractors who have to reinstall everything before we take it again. A perfect, self-sustaining closed-loop domestic industrial model, minimizing dependence on foreign entities who mean us ill fortune."

Serge opened the motel room door.

"Holy shit," said Coleman. "Look at all the copper pipes and wires. You must have stolen all of this in the middle of the night."

"The War on Terror never sleeps."

Coleman high-stepped through the cluttered room. "But with all this copper, why are you upset about the TV news story the other night?"

"Because even the War on Terror has rules. Like, you don't use crowbars to ply the brass plaques off VFW posts that list the names of all the local patriots who have made the supreme sacrifice since the First World War."

"That's not right." Coleman tried the TV. "Can't they just make a new one."

Serge shook his head. "It's a small post. They didn't keep a list of the names. Sounds like an obvious thing to do, but nobody even considered this a distant possibility. The tribute will be gone forever unless we can trace the culprit. I've got eyes on the street."

"That phone call to Manny's Towing and Salvage?"

"If the bastard tries to fence the plaques within twenty miles, we got him."

Coleman changed channels. "What about all this copper?"

"Sell it to Manny. And give him some for his trouble if he comes through."

"No, I mean where'd you get it?"

"Another thing that burns my ass. Florida is one of the few places with a law that says your primary residence can never be seized to pay debts, even if they're the results of criminal fraud or worse. That's why O.J. moved here when he was being sued by the Goldmans. Wall Street fuck-heads regularly liquidate all their assets and buy the biggest home possible before going to jail. Then they get out a few years later and live in a palace, while their swindled retirees eat Kibbles 'n Bits—"

Knock knock knock.

Serge spun and flicked open a switchblade. "What the hell's that?"

Coleman turned up the volume on the news. "The door."

Knock knock knock.

Coleman began going through the room's bureau for loose change. In the second drawer he discovered three prescription bottles and instantly glowed with the kind of dark horse optimism that is only available in the drug culture. His spirits sagged when he realized the bottles were empty, had Serge's name on the labels, and were all for no-fun serotonin-management chemicals. The refill dates bordered on historical. "Serge? When was the last time you took—"

Knock knock knock!

Coleman returned to the TV dial. "Aren't you going to get that?"

"Yes, but not right away. Because it's not just any door." Serge started to tiptoe. "It's the magic door at a fleabag motel. Which means until I open it, the possibilities are infinitely greater than that of other doors we've come to know and love . . ."

Knock knock knock!

Serge continued silently creeping. "No fuckin' boundaries, man! This dump could attract anyone with a limber global outlook. Cadaver dog trainers, pearl divers, snake handlers, snowboarders, celebrity bulimics, Filipino mystics who hang themselves with hooks through their flesh, Blue Öyster Cult, cannibals, and people curious about cannibals."

Coleman fired up a joint. "What if it's a midget?"

"That would work," said Serge. "You open a door and find a midget, and there's no way you can be in a bad mood. It's just not possible."

KNOCK KNOCK KNOCK. *"Dammit, Serge, open up! I'm growing a beard out here!"*

Serge's chin fell to his chest. "Crap." He undid the chain and turned the knob. "Manny, great to see you." Serge stuck his head out the door, glanced suspiciously both ways, then grabbed his guest by the shirt and yanked him off his feet into the room. "Please come in."

Manny looked around the room at all the copper. "You've been a busy boy."

"Terrorism."

"Where'd you get all this?"

Coleman changed the channel again and turned up the volume on another local news program.

"Good evening. This is Pam Swanson outside the water-front mansion of disgraced hedge fund manager Tobias Green-leaf, where police are releasing few details about a brazen overnight break-in . . ."

Manny pointed at the TV. "Greenleaf?"

Serge just smiled.

Manny slapped him on the shoulder. "Should have known." He walked over to a stack of copper coils. "Looks like you hit the a/c units pretty hard." Then he swept an arm back at the rest of the room. "But those straight pipes and wires must have been inside the walls."

"Not anymore," said Serge.

Manny whistled. "Must have taken hours of work hacking through the drywall with axes."

"And a demolition saw."

"*. . . However, unnamed sources describe extensive interior damage at the mansion and estimate repair costs at almost a quarter-million dollars. Off the record, officials speculate the wholesale vandalism could be payback for the hundreds of retirement accounts that were left worthless . . .*"

"You used a demolition saw?" said Manny. "You're not in contracting. How'd you figure out which walls weren't load-bearing?"

"That's easy," said Serge. "Just follow the stress lines of the architecture. It's obvious to anyone with a knack for calculus."

"So you left the copper in those walls behind?"

"No, I figured out a way to get that, too."

Manny scratched his head. "But how would you be able—"

"*. . . Wait, something's happening . . .*" A deep rumbling sound from the TV set. "*. . . There's frantic activity at the west wing of the mansion . . .*" Background shouting. "*Get out! Get out now!*" People running willy-nilly across the lawn. "*. . . Police and fire officials are evacuating the mansion. The roof . . . the whole wing . . . it's collapsing as we speak. . . . Now it's pulling down the center of the building . . . Words cannot begin to describe this scene of devastation, but I'll keep talking anyway . . .*"

Manny turned to Serge and slowly grinned. "I thought this was about copper."

"It was." Serge stopped and smacked himself in the forehead. "I forgot. I never took calculus."

"*. . . Now the east wing has just come down, the whole estate completely flattened. And since all of Greenleaf's assets had been sheltered in the house under Florida's no-seizure law, he's completely wiped out.*"

"*Pam, this is Jim on the anchor desk. Surely someone as smart as Greenleaf would have insurance . . .*"

"*That's correct, Jim. But as soon as the claims check is issued, it's a financial instrument and not a house, which is no longer shielded under the no-seizure law, and will immediately be turned over to the victims whose retirement accounts he wiped out . . .*"

Manny glanced at Serge again. "You planned this all along?"

"Who? Me?"

A hearty laugh. "I got the guys outside. Let's start getting this copper loaded."

The TV screen switched to a local VFW hall. "*. . . In other news, there are no new leads in the heartless theft of memorial plaques to the area's fallen, which has brought out dozens of supporters holding a candlelight vigil . . .*"

A cell phone rang. "Manny here. . . . What? . . . When did this happen? . . . That's great news. . . . I mean it's bad . . . I mean, you know what I mean." He clapped the phone shut. "Serge, that was Nicky the Mooch. Just got word on those plaques of yours. Someone's trying to unload them in Lutz."

"So Nicky's got them?"

Manny shook his head. "Guy's been laying low because of all the heat. But he finally risked going to Nicky's scrap yard because Nicky is, well, like you and me."

"You mean casual with the letter of the law?"

"Nicky said that when he dialed my number a minute ago, the guy must have thought he was calling the cops. He spooked and split."

"Damn," said Serge. "Now we may never get them back."

"Not so fast," said Manny. "He recognized the guy. From time to time, brings in stuff from construction sites. But a month ago, he was actually selling something legitimate. The bumper fell off his car. So he let Nicky copy his driver's license like they're supposed to do the rest of the time. Helps make his logbook look at least half kosher."

Serge pumped his eyebrows. "Nicky's got his address?"

"Just pulled it. He's waiting for your call."

"Can't thank you enough." Serge pointed beside the bed. "That pile of pipes? On me."

"Nice to be back doing business with you." Manny pulled work gloves from his pocket and slipped them on. "So what's going to happen now?"

"Tomorrow's Thanksgiving." Serge retrieved his pistol from a suitcase and checked the magazine. "Only polite thing is to invite him to dinner."

CHAPTER TWO

THE NEXT DAY

South Tampa. The neighborhood was called Palma Ceia. An oasis of pastel bungalows, preserved Mediterraneans, and old Florida ranch houses. Tastefully landscaped with royal palms and bougainvilleas. Kids on sidewalks. Bikes and skateboards. Safe.

The streets had names like Santiago, San Juan, and Sunset Drive. A few blocks in from the bay sat an unassuming road called Triggerfish Lane.

Fourth house on the left. Whitewashed with turquoise trim and, next to the front door, a turquoise sailfish over the address: 888. In the middle of the yard stood an arching date palm that was illuminated after dark with a baby spotlight, but it was only noon, and the tree didn't need attention.

Thanksgiving Day.

Inside, the home was filled with the kind of loving aroma from holiday cooking that makes women think of past family gatherings and makes men want to watch football.

Jim Davenport opened the oven door with pot holders.

"Jim!" whispered Martha. "Your mother's fluffing the cushions!"

"You made a great turkey this year."

"You're not listening!"

"I am." He slid the turkey out. "I just want this to go well."

"And she brought her own stuffing, even though I asked her not to because I had my own recipe. And then she shows up at the door with a bowl and claims she doesn't remember me saying any such thing. She conveniently forgets all my requests."

Jim set the pan on the counter. "Martha—"

"It's passive-aggressive."

"It's stuffing."

"Did you see her stuffing? Hamburger! Who puts meat inside of meat?"

"Let's go sit down . . ."

. . . Silence at the dinner table.

Martha Davenport smiled tensely across the serving platters.

Rita Davenport smiled back and looked at her plate. "Martha, do you need a new dishwasher?"

"Why?"

"Nothing. But remind me to ask you where the bleach is." Then she shifted her eyes. "Jim? Remember the turkey your grandmother used to make? Nothing could compare to her recipe . . . Oh, and by that, I didn't mean anything about your turkey, Martha. I'm sure it's fine. Especially with my stuffing." She placed her napkin in her lap. "Yessiree, his grandmother was quite the cook . . ."

Martha practiced breathing exercises.

"Jim," said Rita. "Have you heard anything from Tommy Kilborne?"

"No, Ma."

"I heard his wife invited his mother to move in with them. Isn't that nice? I don't know what's going to happen to me. I worry that nobody will be there. I was trapped in my bathtub the other day."

"What!" said Jim. "For how long?"

"Just a few seconds this time, but soon, who knows?"

Martha clutched her napkin tightly under the table.

Jim glanced anxiously at both of them. "Ha ha, don't want the food to get cold."

Rita scooted her chair closer to the table. "I always liked Tommy's wife. So generous. Some women could have a problem with their mother-in-law moving in, even if it means leaving them to rot. I have spastic colon." She bowed her head. "Jim, why don't you say grace?"

"I'd much rather hear you give the blessing," said Jim. "It's practically tradition."

"No, I insist."

"Mom, I'm not sure I even remember."

"How can you forget grace if you say it every night?"

"You know I converted years ago."

She briefly waved a hand. "I don't believe that. You know, it's not too late to have the children baptized."

"Mom," said Jim. "Melvin's in college, and Debbie's married."

"What about Nicole. She's still in high school." Rita looked in another direction at a young girl seated at the table, dressed entirely in black with heavy black eye makeup. "Nicole, why are you giggling?"

"Nothing, Grandma." She turned and smiled in her mother's direction.

"Nicole," said Rita Davenport. "Why don't *you* say grace?"

Martha's eyes shot daggers when she saw the grin on her daughter's face: Don't you dare!

Nicole looked back at her grandmother. "I can't say grace."

"Why not, young lady?"

"Because I don't believe in God."

"Ahhhh!" Rita clapped her hands over her ears.

Martha involuntarily shrieked.

Jim lowered his head and sighed.

Nicole cracked up.

Rita Davenport rocked back and forth in her chair. "I didn't hear that! I didn't hear that! Jesus in heaven, the child—she doesn't mean it! . . ."

"Nicole!" shouted Martha. "Tell your grandmother right now you don't mean that!"

The teenager stifled laughs. "Sorry, Grandma. I was only kidding."

"What kind of a joke is that?" Then to Martha: "You approve of this behavior?"

Jim's arms flew out, practically lunging halfway across the table. "Mom, Martha didn't say anything. I'll talk to Nicole later."

Rita turned back to the teen. "Please don't do that again to your sweet grandmother. So, you really do believe in God?"

"Yes." Nicole shot her mom a glance, then back to her grandmother. "But I choose to follow Satan."

"Ahhhhh!" Hands over Rita's ears again.

Martha shrieked.

Jim slowly covered his face with his hands.

Nicole was still cracking up as she rose from the table and headed for the door.

"Where do you think you're going?" yelled Martha.

"To the mall."

"No, you're coming back to this table and sitting down right this minute!"

The door slammed behind the teen.

Rita's hands fell from her ears. "I'll be dead soon."

MEANWHILE . . .

South Dale Mabry Highway.

A '72 Chevelle jumped the curb in front of a sub-budget motel.

"Serge," said Coleman, glancing over his shoulder into the backseat. "That's a pretty big turkey."

"The biggest they had."

"But there's no way we'll be able to eat it all."

"That's the whole point of Thanksgiving!" The Chevelle skidded up to their room. "Cooking way too much friggin' food, cramming the fridge with mountains of leftovers, and then the race is on against salmonella. The most exciting holidays are the ones where not everybody is going to make it."

Coleman opened his door. "You sure we'll go unnoticed at this motel."

"We loaded all that copper, didn't we?"

"Yeah, but then we dragged that tied-up guy from your trunk and into the room."

"Did anyone complain?"

"The guy."

"Besides him?"

"No, but I feel pretty exposed right next to this busy highway."

"Look, if Cuban spies can go unnoticed, we'll blend in like ninjas."

"Spies?"

Serge reached in the backseat and grunted to lift the turkey. "See the military checkpoint down at the end of this road? That's MacDill Air Force Base, home of Central Command. Most people don't realize it, but everything important in the world is coordinated on that tiny tip of land at the south end of the Tampa peninsula. Iraq, Afghanistan, you name it."

"What does that have to do with Cubans?"

Serge waddled toward their door with the giant frozen

bird in his arms. "Back in the nineties, Castro sent spies here to monitor the base. Total farce. Against an installation sealed that tight, what are a few of Fidel's boys going to do? It was all just window dressing so Castro could tell the other Latin leaders, 'Shit yeah, I have people in Tampa.' . . . Coleman, get the door for me?"

Coleman inserted the key and turned the knob. "They didn't spy?"

"No, they starved." Serge entered the room and hit the light switch with his shoulder. "Castro so totally destroyed his island's economy that he couldn't pay them anymore. They ended up pawning their binoculars and taking jobs as dishwashers. And because they were so broke, they lived in motels right along this strip, maybe even this one."

Serge tossed the turkey on the bed and it bounced two feet.

"We're just going to eat the turkey straight?" asked Coleman.

"Of course not." Serge ran back to the car and returned with a large paper sack. "Thanksgiving is why they invented Kentucky Fried Chicken. We got all the fixin's." He began removing items. "Here are the biscuits and super-large sides of mashed potatoes and gravy, macaroni and cheese . . . Doesn't it smell great?"

Coleman turned on the TV. "Football."

Serge dug deeper into the bag. "And the pièce de ré sistance, coleslaw to die for." He tossed the last Styrofoam container to Coleman. "Ice that down in the sink like the Pilgrims did with the Indians."

Coleman went in the bathroom. "But how will we cook the turkey? Everything else is ready."

"Have to eat the turkey later. It's all side dishes until then."

Serge sat down at the desk facing the wall and tucked a napkin in the collar of his T-shirt. Coleman sat next to him, facing the same peeling wall. Serge set his fists on the desk, a plastic utensil gripped upright in each one, and smiled back at his buddy in their crack-den motel. "Now, this is fuckin' tradition."

Coleman dove into the mashed potatoes. He stopped. "Serge, what about the guy?"

"The guy? . . . Oh!" Serge threw his arms up. "My manners!"

He walked across the room, opened the closet, and stared down at a young, hog-tied man with duct tape across his mouth. "You completely slipped my mind. I'm so embarrassed. Come! Join our feast!" Serge dragged him across the carpet.

Coleman munched a biscuit and turned up the TV. "The Dolphins are playing the Lions."

"The Dolphins?" Serge let go of the hostage and wandered over. "I love the Dolphins! What's the score?"

"Don't know." *Munch, munch.*

Serge pulled up a chair in front of the TV. "It's third and long. Pick up the blitz! Pick up the blitz! . . . Ooo, they didn't pick up the blitz."

Coleman pushed the rest of the biscuit into his mouth and popped another Pabst. "What's that noise?"

Serge's nose was practically against the TV screen. "What noise?"

"*That* noise."

Serge turned the volume down. "I hear it . . ." He turned around. "Oh, forgot about him again. Just left him on his belly. My attention span."

"Because you stopped taking your meds."

"Exactly. I like my attention span." Serge got up from his chair. "Lets me juggle multiple tasks and get more accomplished. Follow the space program, work on my total solution for the Middle East, thwart customer-service people who make up answers, determine if fifteen minutes really can save me fifteen percent, develop renewable energy source from golf balls lost in ponds, retrieve priceless brass plaques . . ."

"That guy's wiggling around the floor pretty good for someone hog-tied," said Coleman. "I think he's trying to say something."

"Probably wants to tell us what side dishes he wants." Serge leaned down and ripped the duct tape off the captive's mouth.

"Ow!"

Serge smiled with big white teeth and held a Styrofoam container under the man's nose. "Good coleslaw! Nobody makes it like KFC. Go ahead, have the rest."

"Serge," said Coleman. "Doesn't he need plastic utensils?"

"No, I'll just set it on the floor in front of his mouth."

"Please!" said the hostage. "Don't hurt me!"

"Hurt you?" said Serge. "Why would I do that? Oh, I know. Like when we came to your apartment last night and requested the plaques back. And if I remember, I asked real nice, too. I might have said 'cocksucker' a few times, but that's always taken out of context. And what did you do? First, you cut my friend with a knife . . ."

Coleman held up his arm, showing a fresh bandage on a flesh wound.

" . . . Then you pulled a gun on me. Luckily I had pulled mine first. Even then, I didn't take your style of hospitality personally. But what crossed the line was when I tried to reason with you about the importance of those plaques— real nice again—explaining the difference between them and air-conditioning coils, and what did you say about the people whose names were engraved?" Serge got out his gun again and tapped his chin in thought. "Yeah, I remember now. 'Fuck 'em.'" He shook his head. "Not good. That's the problem with this generation. No sense of history. They haven't the foggiest notion of all the sacrifices that have been made so they can safely lounge about this country texting and tweeting . . ."

The man began whimpering.

"Not the crying again," said Serge. "Obviously you don't know anything about me. I take the high road. The answer isn't to attack you. Our nation's too divided for that. No, the constructive remedy is to educate you and welcome you into the program. It's Thanksgiving! So I've invited you here today as my guest, to break bread and celebrate the men and women on those plaques. Look around you! This room is chock-full of liberty. Some mold, but more liberty."

Coleman raised a beer. "Pursuit of happiness."

Serge nodded. "And pursuit of happiness." He replaced the tape on the captive's mouth and clapped his hands a single time. "You hungry? Let's start getting that turkey ready!"

"But, Serge," said Coleman. "How are we going to cook it? There's nothing in here."

"Got it covered."

Serge grabbed his car keys and ran outside to the trunk of the Chevelle. He came back carrying a large metal device, and kicked the door closed behind him with his foot.

"What's that?" asked Coleman.

Serge carefully set it down next to the plaque burglar. "Remember that menu of Florida newspaper headlines that keep repeating themselves every holiday season?"

"Yeah?"

"This is one I forgot to mention." Serge reached inside for a page of safety instructions and tossed it over his shoulder. "Hand me that turkey."

THREE HOURS LATER

A dozen police cars converged in the parking lot of a sub-budget motel on South Dale Mabry Highway near the air-force base. Yellow crime tape. Forensic team.

A white Crown Vic rolled up. The detectives got out and stared at the incinerated and gutted room.

A stretcher rolled out the door with a covered body, still smoldering.

The lead investigator approached the sergeant in charge. "What have we got here? Another meth-lab explosion?"

The sergeant took off his hat and wiped his forehead. "That's what we thought at first."

"What else could possibly have caused it? In all my years, I've only seen destruction this total at drug labs."

"You know those same newspaper headlines you see every year? Floridians trying to keep warm by barbecuing indoors?"

"He was barbecuing?" The detective watched them load the stretcher into the back of a coroner's truck. "What an idiot."

"Not barbecuing. We found a large deep fryer in the room. And a big turkey. There won't be leftovers."

"Deep-frying a turkey?" The detective looked back at the room. "But a grease fire wouldn't cause that kind of damage. The door's blown off the hinges and charred like a briquet."

"Wasn't your average grease fire. Forensics hasn't officially ruled, but it's looking like they were deep-frying a frozen turkey."

"Jesus, you never deep-fry a frozen turkey. It goes off like a bomb. A big one." The detective opened a notebook and shook his head. "Well, like you said about those headlines, every year, two, or three. This guy really was an idiot."

"Or a genius," said the sergeant.

The detective stopped writing. "What are you talking about? . . . Wait a minute. You said 'they' were deep-frying. I thought there was only one body."

The sergeant held up an evidence bag. Melted nylon cord. "Our friend was hog-tied. He had some help in there with the basting."

"You mean this was a murder? But what kind of sick—"

A uniformed officer trotted over, finishing a conversation on his walkie-talkie. "Sir, we just got a report from the VFW hall. Someone returned those stolen plaques."

"Great," said the sergeant. "But what's that got to do with this?"

"They left a note. An apology. Maybe not, I don't know. But there was a driver's license, and the address of this motel room. We might have just ID'd the victim."

The sergeant glanced sideways at the detective. "Score one for the good guys."

The detective stuck his notebook back in his jacket. "Send me the case report. I'll make sure it gets filed under a very tall stack of papers."

CHAPTER THREE

THREE WEEKS LATER

Christmas songs. A line of small children waiting to see Santa. Others sitting on a foam mat watching a puppet show.

"This new mall's unbelievable," said Jim Davenport, walking past the Gap. "Look at the ice-skating rink."

"I hate this time of year," said Martha Davenport.

"But look at all the kids having fun."

"We had to park a mile away, not to mention the insane traffic on the way over."

"Martha, it's the holidays." They continued along the upper level past kiosks for cell phones and sunglasses.

"Wouldn't be so bad if I didn't have to shop for your mother. She returns everything, you know."

"Not everything."

"You're right. She prominently displays anything *you* get her. That's an attack on me."

A group of gleeful children with colorful balloons ran by shrieking.

"Martha, you're letting her get under your skin."

"I'm dreading this next visit."

"But we have to visit," said Jim. "It's Christmas."

"God, that last visit. Can you believe what Nicole said?"

"Because she sees how my mom gets to you."

"That makes it okay? Like it's sport to her?"

"No, it was terrible," said Jim. "I grounded her, remember?"

"Lot of good that did. She just kept going out. You're not firm enough with her. And now she wants a tattoo!"

"I'll sit down and talk to her."

"Be firm this time."

They went into the Apple store. The balloon kids shrieked by the entrance, followed by two elves, one tall and thin with ice-blue eyes, the other short and pudgy with a round, non-intellectual-looking head.

"Serge," said Coleman. "Are we shopping?"

"No, I just love coming to the mall at Christmas, digging how stores tap into the whole holiday spirit, especially the bookstores with their special bargain displays."

"Displays?" asked Coleman.

"Big ones near the front," said Serge. "If you want to show someone you put absolutely zero thought into their gift, you buy a giant picture book about steam locomotives, ceramic thimbles, or Scotland."

"But why are we wearing elf suits?"

"To spread good cheer."

"What for?"

"Because of the War on Christmas."

"Who started the war?" asked Coleman.

"Ironically, the very people who coined the term and claim *others* started the war. They're upset that people of different faiths, along with the coexistence crowd who respect those faiths, are saying 'Season's Greetings' and 'Happy Holidays.' But nobody's stopping anyone from saying 'Merry Christmas.'"

"And they're still mad?"

Serge shrugged. "It's the new holiness: Tolerance can't be tolerated. So they hijack the birth of Jesus as a weapon to start quarrels and order people around. Christmas should be about the innocence of children—and adults reverting to children to rediscover their innocence. That's why we're in elf suits. We're taking Christmas back!"

"So how do we spread this good cheer?"

"Maybe by skipping. Let's try skipping. You see someone skipping, and you wish wars would stop. Children skip all the time, but you become an adult and forget to skip. Let's skip."

"Wait up!" Coleman skipped alongside Serge. "But I still don't get this elf thing. How can we be elves if the mall didn't hire us?"

"And that's what everyone thinks." Serge skipped and waved at curious shoppers. "But there's no law that says you can't just unilaterally decide to be an elf, buy a costume, and hit the mall. That's the whole key to life: Fuck the conventional wisdom on elves."

"So then that makes us . . ."

"That's right: wildcat elves."

"But, Serge, what if someone says something?"

"What are they going to say?" Serge stopped skipping. "It's like clipboards. You walk around all smart and serious, writing on a clipboard, and people stand back in respect. Or orange cones. You can buy them at any Home Depot. Then you set them out according to your needs, and the public thinks, 'He must be official. He's got orange cones.' Those are the Big Three: clipboards, orange cones, elf suits. People don't question . . . I need coffee. There's the Coffee Circus."

The Davenports emerged from the Apple store. Outside, a line of small children stood in fear against a wall. Their balloons floated to the ceiling. Tears rolled down little cheeks.

A mall cop pointed at them menacingly and shouted. "Stop running and screaming! This is a mall, not a playground! If I catch you again—"

"Hey!" yelled Martha Davenport. "Don't talk to them like that!"

"Are you one of their parents?" demanded the security guard.

"No, but there's no reason—"

"Then butt out!"

Martha stepped forward. "What did you just say to me?"

Jim tugged her sleeve. "Martha . . ."

The mall cop leaned into her face. "I said, butt out!"

"Or you'll what?"

Jim tugged her sleeve. "Martha . . ."

The mall cop sneered. "Or I'll toss you out of the mall!"

"Excuse me," said Jim. "Please don't talk to my wife like that."

"I'll toss you out, too!"

Martha stormed off.

"Martha! . . ." yelled Jim. He ran and caught up to her as she walked briskly past the Jelly Bean Barn. "Martha, where are you going?"

"I'm going to report him."

"But he's a mall cop."

"Oh, big position of authority."

"No, that's the point. Mall security sometimes attracts a certain type. And that guy demonstrated he has an authority complex. What if he gets fired?"

"That's what I want to happen!"

"But who knows what kind of retaliation he'll take. He clearly has impulse problems."

"You could use some impulse problems."

Jim did his best to keep up with her raging stride. "But I'm out of town a lot on business. I don't want to worry about you and Nicole while I'm gone."

"It'll be an anonymous report."

"But what if he finds out?"

"He won't. It's anonymous."

"It was anonymous when you reported those neighbors with the washing machines and motorcycles in their yard. They weren't even living on our street. I don't understand—"

"It was against code. We keep a nice house and pay taxes."

"But the code people accidentally gave them a copy of

your anonymous report," said Jim. "Didn't the motorcycles give you a clue? They were bikers! They came to the door. I had to talk my way out of it."

"It was the code people's fault for giving them that report. I reported them."

"And for the next year we got cited for every little branch that fell out of the yard waste container."

"I'm still reporting that guy," said Martha. "Here's the mall office." She turned and marched down a stark corridor, past the restrooms, toward a series of plain doors.

Jim called after her: "I'll wait here."

"Suit yourself."

Jim's heart rate rocketed from the stress. Under his breath: "Relax. Count to ten . . ."

From behind: "Jim! Jim Davenport!"

Jim turned around. "Ahhhhhhh!"

Two elves approached. "Jim, it's me, Serge. And you remember Coleman."

Jim backed up. "Don't come any closer!"

"Is that any way to greet a dear old friend?"

Jim glanced back and forth, then grabbed Serge by the arm and hustled him out of sight from the opening of the corridor. "I can't let Martha see you."

"Martha's with you? I'd love to say hi."

"No!" Jim put up his hands. "Serge, I realize you mean well. But please leave us alone. Martha still hasn't gotten over the last stuff."

"Did I conduct myself badly? I mean, yeah, gunfire and a few very tiny explosions, but I love you guys!" Serge scanned the crowd of shoppers. "Where is the little lady?"

"Down the hall in the manager's office." Jim peeked around the corner. "Reporting a mall cop."

"What for?"

"Screaming at little kids and making them cry."

"What were they doing?"

"Running and laughing."

"What an asshole!"

"And he said some nasty things to Martha."

"What!" said Serge.

"I tried speaking to him, but—"

Serge placed a consoling hand on Jim's shoulder. "I know you did."

Jim looked down at his shoes. "Sometimes I think I should be more aggressive. The disrespectful way he talked to my wife . . ."

Serge squeezed his shoulder and shook his head. "No, Jim. Stay the way you are. You're one of the good guys. I'm sure you did everything appropriate to defend Martha's honor."

Jim looked up. "You think so?"

Serge nodded hard, taking a sip of his extra-large coffee from the Coffee Circus. "Absolutely." Then he stopped and rubbed his nose. "Except this mall-cop thing is tricky business. They attract certain types, authority complex. He might get ahold of the anonymous report."

"That's exactly what I told Martha . . . Wait—" Jim pointed toward the other side of the pavilion. "There he is now."

"Who?"

"The mall cop. Next to the Pretzel Emporium."

"I see him," said Serge. "He's yelling at more kids."

Jim puffed up his chest. "Maybe I should say something."

Serge grabbed his shoulder again. "Jim, you're still pure. This is my territory . . . Come on, Coleman. Put down the beer. We're rolling . . ."

"Serge, wait," said Jim. "What are you going to . . ."

But they had already taken off.

From the office corridor: "Jim."

"Ahhhhh! . . . Oh, it's you."

"Of course it's me," said Martha. "Why are you so jumpy? Did I hear you talking to someone around the corner?"

"No, nothing, what?"

"You're acting kind of suspicious."

"So how did the report go?"

"The assistant mall manager that I was supposed to see was out, so I left a message with his secretary for him to call . . . There he is now."

"The manager?"

"No, that mall cop." Martha nodded in the direction of the other side of the escalators. "Look at that cocky asshole . . . That's odd."

"What?"

"Two guys just passed him going the other way. Then they made a quick U-turn, and are right behind him stride for stride. Seems they're following him."

"Who is?"

"Those two elves. Now they've started skipping."

Jim coughed and hit himself in the center of his chest. "W-w-what elves?"

"How can you not notice them? The one on the left is the tallest elf I've ever seen, with the giant coffee . . . Does he seem familiar to you? I could swear I've seen him somewhere before."

"Ahhh!" Jim put his arm around Martha and turned her the other way.

She tried looking back. "Jim, what's gotten into you?"

"I know what you need," he said with a crooked smile. "How about some ice cream? There's the food court."

"Jim, why do you always think a woman just needs ice cream to put her in a better mood?"

"It doesn't?"

"No, it's true. Where'd you see the ice cream parlor?"

The uniform was spiffy. Navy blue with eagles on the shoulders. The mall cop kept it pressed. And maintained his mustache like Magnum, P.I. His forearms were conspicuously thick from gym workouts. If a hot babe had a lot of bags, he always offered assistance, and they always declined. As they walked away, he took their pictures with his cell phone. In his pocket was a set of keys for various mall doors and a black Delta 88 parked outside in the employee lot.

The guard strolled casually past Banana Republic and Foot Locker. But his senses were keen, on the watch for any mall infraction. He thought: *I have to go to the bathroom.*

The mall cop pushed open a door and walked across black-and-white-checkered tiles. He unzipped and hummed to himself, making a game of hitting the urinal cake.

The door opened behind him. The ever-vigilant guard reflexively glanced over his shoulder. He chuckled a single time. Losers. When his business was finished, the guard zipped back up and turned around.

"Excuse me," said Serge.

"What do *you* want?"

"For you to stop being mean to little children and decent women."

"What the hell are you talking about?"

"I've been watching you."

"*You've* been watching *me*?" The guard shoved Serge in the chest. "I'm so going to have you fired. I'm heading to the office right now."

"You can't get me fired." Serge raised his extra-large coffee, draining it in one large guzzle, then whipping the empty cup sideways at the garbage can. "I don't work at the mall."

The guard stopped with a confused look. "But you're wearing an elf suit."

"I fuck conventional wisdom's wife. Clipboard. Orange cones. You're a mall cop. Not a real cop. My personal code is never harm real cops, who risk their lives every day. The Thin Blue Line. You're an almost-cop, so harming you is a gray area. Thin Gray Line? Who knows? So I'll err on the side of decency and ask nice. Don't yell at any more kids before you're fired."

"Fired?"

"And after you're fired, let it go. Don't look for the anonymous complaint that got you dismissed. And if you somehow do find the anonymous complaint, don't go after the Davenports, which isn't their name. Brass plaques, frozen turkey, LEGOs. I'll be watching. That is all. You may go."

"You're insane! . . . and dead!" The guard began rolling up his sleeves. "Both of you."

"You can't hit me. I'm in an elf suit. I'm calling it."

"Oh, I can't hit you, eh?"

"No, look, see? Elf hat." Serge took the hat off, twirled it on his left index finger, then his right, then quickly placed it over the guard's face and smashed his fist as hard as he could in his nose. Plus a knee to the groin. The guard went down like a sack of concrete, clipping his chin on the edge of the porcelain and sending two teeth into the urinal cake.

Thus Serge began a vicious stomping—kidneys, ribs, spleen—kicking away with hands on his hips like a demented river dance. Coleman peed on the guard.

"Coleman, watch out! You're hitting my elf shoes!"

"Sorry."

A final kick in the throat. "Don't you ever be mean to kids again! And stay away from the Davenports, who are called something else."

The mall cop's face lay sideways on the tiles. Blood streaming from his nose and mouth, finally managing to open his eyelids a slit, seeing four green elf shoes walking out the door to the sound of the jingle bells on their curled-up toes.

CHAPTER FOUR

TRIGGERFISH LANE

A phone rang.

"I got it." Jim Davenport set down tools to hang a painting and picked up the receiver. "Hello? . . . Yes, this is the Davenports' . . . Uh-huh, right, we were there yesterday . . . What? . . . No, we don't know anything about that . . . I see . . . That's unusual . . . I don't know; I'll have to ask her . . ."

"Who is it?" Martha yelled from the kitchen.

"Excuse me a second." Jim covered the phone. "It's the mall."

"What do they want?"

"About your complaint. They got your message and want to talk."

"Good." Martha walked out of the kitchen, drying her hands on a dish towel. "I'm glad to see at least someone takes this sort of thing seriously."

"I think they're actually more interested in something else. That mall cop is in the hospital. They suspect some kind of fight in a restroom, although he's claiming he was attacked. They've put him on suspension until they finish the investigation."

"What does that have to do with me?"

"You left your complaint about the same time. They just want to know what you might have seen."

Martha held out her hand. "Let me talk to him . . . Hello? Yes, this is Martha Davenport . . . But it will be completely confidential, right? . . . Okay, I saw him behaving unprofessionally toward a group of small children. And he was extremely rude to me . . . No, nothing about any attack . . . Well, who does he say attacked him? . . . Elves? . . ."

Jim fell into a chair, knocking over a lamp.

"Jim, are you okay?"

"Just slipped . . . I'll get the dustpan. Don't step on the lightbulb pieces."

Back into the phone: "No, I'm still here . . . As a matter of fact I do remember some elves . . . Yeah, and I was remarking to my husband that they seemed to be following him . . . A tall one and a chubby one . . . What do you mean your mall doesn't employ elves? I wasn't seeing things . . . Could you repeat that last part? . . . The guard claims the elves mentioned our name? That's weird . . ."

Jim returned with the dustpan. Martha covered the phone. "Jim, they say the elves mentioned our name." Then into the phone: "I'll have to call you back. There's something wrong with my husband. But I demand that man be fired for his earlier behavior, regardless of your investigation."

She hung up and set the phone down. "Jim, you look like you're having a stroke. What's going on?"

Jim let go of the wall. "Just some saliva went down my windpipe."

Martha headed back to the kitchen, eyeing Jim as she went. "You've been acting awfully strange lately."

Jim craned his neck and watched until she'd disappeared around the corner. Then he ran both hands through his hair. "Whew. That was close." He picked up his tools to screw in the anchor bolt for the painting.

The doorbell rang.

"I got it." He set down a screwdriver and answered the door.

"Jim!"

"Ahhhh!"

Jim jumped out onto the porch and slammed the door behind him. Frantic whispering: "Serge, what are you doing here? You can't let Martha see you!"

"I brought a welcome basket!" Serge raised it by the wicker handle. "It's got cellophane and fake grass and everything. There's the cheese wheel—"

"Serge! I've got to get you off the porch before Martha comes out here!"

"Why?" asked Serge. "Are you in some kind of trouble?"

The door opened. "Jim, who rang the—"

Serge smiled and raised his eyebrows. "Surprise! And,

Martha, may I say you're radiant? . . . You remember Coleman . . ."

A slight wave from Serge's pal. *Burp.*

"Jim!" snapped Martha. "What are they doing here?"

Serge smiled and held up the basket again. "Cellophane and fake grass . . ."

"Jim! Get them the hell off our property this minute!"

"Look," said Serge. "If Jim did something to get in the shithouse with you, I'm sure there's a perfect explanation."

"Jim!"

A deep, pounding sound came up the street. The bass line from "Bad Romance."

A low-riding GTX with gold rims pulled up to the curb. Nicole necked briefly with the driver, then got out. The sports car screeched away.

Martha marched halfway down the porch steps. "Nicole! Is that the same boy I told you—"

The teen brushed past her. "I'm getting a tattoo."

Martha's eyes darted between Serge and her daughter disappearing into the house. Twin crises. She made the call and ran inside "Nicole! Come back here! . . ."

"Whoa!" said Coleman.

"Holy fuck," Serge told Jim. "I didn't know what you were up against. Each month when their periods get in sync, you must be juggling chain saws."

"You talking about my wife and daughter . . . ?"

"Just sayin'."

"Please don't."

Serge bowed his head once in respect. "Fair enough.

I haven't been there myself, so the period thing could be touchy—"

"Serge!" Jim stepped close and whispered: "What on earth did you do to that mall cop?"

Serge took a step back, mouth agape, and placed a hand over his heart. "Jim, I'm shocked. I show up with a welcome basket, and we're chatting all friendly about periods and shit, and then suddenly accusations."

Jim idly rubbed his left shoe on the welcome mat. "I'm sorry."

"Don't be." Serge threw an arm around Jim's shoulders. "Meanwhile, it looks like Martha's having some trouble with your daughter. Let's see if I can help. I'm great with kids."

"I think it's a bad idea."

"Don't be silly." He led Jim inside and called down the hall. "Martha! Nicole! It's Serge to the rescue . . ."

TWO MINUTES LATER

Serge and Coleman dashed down the porch steps at 888 Triggerfish Lane. A frying pan flew after them and took a divot out of the lawn. "Don't ever come back!"

They jumped into the Chevelle. "Hurry up and start the car," said Coleman. "She's looking for something else to throw."

Feet ran down the front steps.

"Hurry!" yelled Coleman.

"That's not Martha."

Nicole sprinted down to the car.

"What are you doing?" yelled Serge.

"Coming with you. I'm getting the fuck out of this hell house!"

"Your mouth!" said Serge.

She grabbed the passenger-door handle before Serge could hit the lock button, and dove in the backseat.

"Get out of the car," said Serge.

She pointed up the street. "Just hit the gas."

"Out of the car—"

Martha came running down the steps.

A cast-iron pressure cooker crashed and creased the Chevelle's hood. "My car! It's vintage!"

"Told you to hit the gas."

Serge peeled out.

Martha ended up in the middle of the street behind the car, throwing her shoes.

Nicole was twisted around in her seat, looking out the rear window and giggling. She turned back around. "That was cool."

"That was not . . . What do you think you're doing?"

Nicole lit a Marlboro Light. "What?"

Serge snatched it away and threw it out the window.

"Hey!"

"Jesus, you're just a kid!" said Serge. "What, sixteen?"

"Fifteen."

Coleman fired a new doobie and passed it back over the front seat. "Wanna hit?"

"Sure." Nicole reached.

Serge slapped his hand. "Coleman! That's illegal!"

"Sorry. How 'bout a beer?"

"No!" yelled Serge. "She's just a kid!"

Nicole pointed. "Is that a real gun?"

"What?" said Serge. "Oh, this? Didn't realize I'd gotten it out again. Something to keep my hands busy."

"Can I hold it?"

"No!" He stowed it under the seat.

Nicole slumped in disappointment. "You guys looked like you were going to be fun."

"We are fun," said Serge. "Ask anyone. Well, not anyone. You know how some people automatically don't like you for no reason?"

The Chevelle made a right for the Gandy Bridge.

"So where are we going, anyway?" asked Nicole.

"We drive around," said Serge. "Waiting for duty to call."

"I get it." Nicole nodded. "You like to go cruisin'. Me, too. Driving around getting messed up. Then maybe street-racing on the Courtney Campbell or Twenty-second causeway. Some of those dudes have guns, too."

"What dudes?"

"Like my boyfriend."

"I've been meaning to talk to you about him," said Serge.

Nicole got out her cell phone. "You mean Snake?"

"Is that a name?"

"No, it's just what the guys at work call him."

"Work?" said Serge. "Like an after-school job."

"No, he dropped out his senior year. Has a job at the Gas-N-Grub."

"Senior?" said Serge. "How old is this Snake?"

"Eighteen."

Serge slapped his forehead. "Now we really have to talk. How many piercings does he have, anyway?"

"Don't be old-fashioned."

"Oh, I don't have a problem with it. They're meant to attract attention, and they attracted mine . . ."

The Chevelle ramped up the bridge over Tampa Bay.

Serge glanced as the young girl tapped her cell phone. "Nicole, what are you doing?"

"Texting." *Tap, tap, tap.*

"But I'm talking to you."

Not looking up: "I hear you." *Tap, tap, tap.*

Serge yanked the phone away.

"Hey!"

"It's rude," said Serge.

"Everybody does it."

"And that's the whole problem with this country today. No manners." Serge unscrewed a thermos of coffee. "People used to hang out and actually communicate. But today they head to the mall and sit together at the Yogurt A Go-Go in their own separate spheres of mobile devices."

"What's wrong with that?"

"It's destroying the art of conversation!" said Serge. "I *love* conversations!"

"Why?"

"Because we're all crazy!" said Serge. "And that's how society makes progress: imaginations getting together and glancing off each other in accidental tangents of invention."

"*That* sounds crazy," said Nicole.

"Think about it." Serge chugged from his coffee thermos. "We all know how schizophrenics talk from our time on the streets interacting with the underpass community, and we're thinking, 'Jesus, I'm glad I'm not like this loopy guy jabbering about time travel, drone aircrafts, and guilt-free dog treats.' . . . But that's only because we're not aware of how our own conversations sound because we're inside them. It's like you don't know your own voice unless you have a tape recorder. And if you *did* have a tape recorder, and recorded a hundred different conversations in a restaurant, where people at leisure have no agenda other than to enjoy each other's company, the chitchat is all over the road, jumping from topic to topic until it's miles from where it began, which nobody can remember. In movies, the talk is a logical straight line, moving plot from A to B. But in real life, it starts with the weather, then office gossip, vacation plans, childhood mishaps, a funny story about a trombone, the benefits of testing batteries with your tongue, why Esperanto never took off, what about Morey Amsterdam?—the heartbreak of psoriasis, the trouble with Tribbles, the thrill is gone, fashion disasters throughout history, turtle migration, my bologna has a first name, you're soaking in Palmolive, then suddenly Einstein blurts out something about the decay of matter and, boom, Nagasaki . . . So how 'bout it?" Serge looked over at Nicole. "Want to try a real human conversation where people actually listen? I'll go first. the Ice Age. Your thoughts?"

"I want my cell phone back."

Serge's head fell back with a sigh. "Okay, then I want to talk about Snake."

"What about him?"

"You two were making out at the curb in front of your house."

"So what?"

"He was being very disrespectful to your parents." Serge wagged a finger. "The kind of man you deserve would walk you to the door and greet your mother and father."

"How do you know my parents, anyway?"

"Me and Jim go way back, through thick and thin."

"I heard some of the stories when I wasn't supposed to. My mom really hates you."

"Because she doesn't understand me. But she's a good woman, and you need to show her gratitude."

"I'm just surprised you and my dad are friends."

"Why do you say that?"

"Because you guys are cool. You're not afraid of anything." Nicole looked out across the passing water. "And my dad is, you know, a little on the wimpy side."

Serge hit the brakes with both feet. A long, tire-screeching stop at the top of the bridge. He turned to Nicole with a mask of rage she had never seen before. "Jim is not wimpy!"

Nicole retreated as far as she could and sank against the passenger door.

"Your dad is one of the most courageous people I know! You think guns and liquor and dope and an excellent car is cool? Well, it is. But your dad has chosen to take on responsibilities I could never dream of . . ."

Car horns blared behind them. Coleman stuck his arm

out the window with a beer in his hand, waving in a "go around" motion.

" . . . There's a war against women going on!" yelled Serge. "Not political. Just men. And your dad has dedicated his life to protect you and your mother from all of them. Next to that, I'm the wimp! . . . Do . . . you . . . understand . . . little . . . girl!"

"Okay, okay, yes. Jesus, I didn't realize you two were so close."

"He's my hero. I want to be just like him."

"Really?"

Serge nodded. "Sorry about freaking you out there for a minute, but I'm sensitive about this."

Nicole's breathing was coming back down. "No biggie."

"I'll make you a deal," said Serge. "Jim needs your help and love in his struggle. Do me a favor and show him respect."

"Why not?"

"That's better."

"But you said a deal," countered Nicole. "What do I get?"

"Back at the house, I heard something about you wanting a tattoo?"

"Oh man, my mom will really hate you."

"No, she won't. I know how to handle women like her." Serge hit the gas again. "You leave that to me."

"I don't think you really know my mom. She'll go ape."

"It's all about the art of conflict. Most people go in head-first." Serge made a skirting gesture with his right hand. "Whereas I outflank."

"You're going to sneak up on my mom?"

"In a manner of speaking." Serge took another swig from his coffee thermos. "Give you an example: the Positive Protest."

"Positive?"

"Say you've got some kind of protest group that wants concessions from the powers that be. But the conflict is going nowhere. So the only option is to take to the streets, creating a massive public disturbance of anarchy that brings the city to its knees. Except for some reason, the city is the only one with a riot squad. Don't ask why, it's just the way they set it up at the beginning. And they come storming in with shields and helmets and batons, sweeping you off the pavement like autumn leaves."

"I've seen it on TV."

"That's where they all go wrong. If I was in charge of the mob, I'd stage a Positive Protest. And when the shock troops start goose-stepping in with the tear gas, you begin waving signs and yelling slogans demanding higher police salaries. Then their bullhorns blare for you to disperse, and you say you totally agree with what they're asking, and it's a shame that the people who have to make you disperse don't receive better benefits and pensions— and that your group will vote en masse for any politician who jacks up their compensation. The riot team can do nothing but stand mute. I'm dying to try it out! Except I don't have a cause yet . . . I could always phone in my grievances later . . ."

"What's that got to do with my tattoo?"

"You'll see when we get there." Serge passed the dog track and pulled into a strip mall. "Because of your age, you'll need parental consent. That's me; they never check. Plus I know this guy."

"Wow, you're really going to help me get a tattoo. That's so cool."

TRIGGERFISH LANE

The front door opened.

Martha came racing out of the kitchen. "Where on earth have you been?"

"Out." Nicole walked by with a sullen expression.

"I want more of an answer than that," said Martha. "Did they hurt you?"

"Don't be lame."

As Nicole left the living room, Martha happened to glance down below the small of her daughter's back. A tiny bit of ink peeked out above the waistband of her shorts. An audible gasp. "A tattoo! . . . Jim, come quick; it's Nicole! It's an emergency!"

Jim ran out of the den. "What's the matter? Is she okay?"

"She got a tattoo."

"I thought she needed parental permission to get one."

"She's got one."

"What is it?"

"Does it matter?" Martha stomped down the hall to a closed bedroom door. She tried the knob. Locked. Pounded with fists. "Open the door this instant! You're in so much trouble!"

The door didn't open. Thumping rock music inside. Joan Jett.

"*. . . Hello Daddy, hello Mom, I'm your ch-ch-ch-cherry bomb . . .*"

Martha turned. "Jim?"

"What? Kick the door in?"

"No, get a key." Martha kept pounding.

"Where's the key?"

"I don't know." More pounding. "Try the junk drawer."

"I'll go look."

Before he could leave, the door opened. "What's all the racket out here?"

"*. . . Don't give a damn 'bout my bad reputation . . .*"

"You got a tattoo!"

"So?"

"We forbid you! And we didn't give any permission!"

Nicole shrugged. "Serge got it for me. He's really cool."

"Serge!" snapped Martha. She began strangling something invisible in midair. "I'll kill him. He disfigured our daughter!"

"You're such a drama queen," said Nicole.

"Turn around immediately!" said Martha. "I want to see what that monster did to you!"

"No!"

Martha looked sideways. "Jim!"

"Nicole," said her father. "Turn around."

The teen opened her mouth. But then remembered her promise to Serge. "Okay, Dad."

She turned around, lifting her shirt and pulling the waistband down an inch.

The parents leaned in for a close inspection.

There it was, just below the tan line. A word in feminine cursive script:

Family.

Nicole dropped her shirt and turned around to face them again. "Satisfied?"

Her parents stood mute.

"Serge also told me to be more grateful for you guys. Whatever."

Nicole went back in her room and closed the door.

CHAPTER FIVE

THE NEXT DAY

Coleman burped. "Look at this line." He stuck his head around the side in an attempt to see the front. "It's like Disney."

"Maybe longer," said Serge, licking a stamp.

"We drove like forever to get here, and now . . . where are we? This is the middle of nowhere."

"Twenty miles east of Orlando to be exact."

Coleman strained his neck for a view of the counter. "But what's the point?"

"Because Florida doesn't get snow, we have a chronic inferiority complex when it comes to Christmas." Serge handed Coleman a stamp. "So we overcompensate: Santa Claus on water skis, on Jet Skis, on surfboards, Christmas cards with barefoot Santas in beach chairs drinking beer, inflatable snowmen, reindeer in tropical shirts, town celebrations where they bring in special machines that shred ice and blow out fake snow that melts immediately and makes the children cry . . . But this place just might be the weirdest."

"What is it?"

"The post office in the city of Christmas, Florida, where thousands descend each year to get their holiday cards postmarked. It's the best tradition we got, so fuck it, I'm rodeo-riding this cultural mutation."

"Why's it called Christmas?" Coleman licked his own stamp. "They have a big celebration way back or something?"

"No," said Serge. "On the twenty-fifth of December, 1837, they began construction of Fort Christmas to fight the Second Seminole War. Nothing says the 'Prince of Peace' like a military installation."

"Who are we mailing your card to?"

"Me," said Serge. "It's got a bitchin' cool Florida postmark. I tried to think who might appreciate it more but drew a blank."

Coleman looked at his own envelope. "Mine's addressed to me, also."

"I did that."

"But when I open this, there'll be no surprise."

"You won't remember," said Serge.

"What's this address, anyway?"

"You'll find out after we drive back to Tampa." Serge used the envelope to fan himself in the heat. "A *lot* of people will be surprised."

Jim Davenport packed a fake-leather briefcase. "Sure feels good to be back on Triggerfish Lane."

"It's not like we had a choice," said Martha. "We were upside down on the house."

Jim shuffled papers into a file. "The economy hit everyone. We came out better than most."

"I liked Davis Islands better." Martha cradled a large mixing bowl and stirred. "This just doesn't feel . . . as safe."

Jim snapped the latches shut on his briefcase. "This neighborhood's perfectly safe. Kids play in the street, neighbors know each other . . ."

Martha stopped stirring. "And remember what happened last time we lived here?"

"So there was a little crime." Jim grabbed the handle of his attaché. "We also had our problems on the island."

Stirring again. "Where are you off to?"

"Work."

"It's one in the afternoon."

"You know my job has odd hours." He gave her a quick kiss. "I won't be back for dinner."

"I'll cover a plate in the fridge."

"Love you . . ."

Jim indeed worked strange hours. And it was true the Davenports had fared the economic downturn better than most. Those two facts went hand in hand. There are opportunities in even the worst economies. Jim had caught one.

He was a consultant.

His company was called Sunshine Solutions, and his

specialty was everything. Didn't matter the industry—manufacturing, hospitality, transportation—Jim got all the biggest accounts.

Not because he had broad experience. He actually knew squat about most of the accounts. In fact, he seemed like the most ill-suited person to offer any kind of advice whatsoever. Which is why he was perfect.

"You're perfect," said the executive who hired him after his interview. "Here's your first account."

"But I don't know anything about hospital administration."

"You don't need to."

"Then how am I supposed to consult?"

"You're not," said the exec. "We're in the consulting business. We don't consult."

"What do we do?"

"Fire people. It's what our clients pay us for. When heads need to roll, they want the ax in the hands of someone who doesn't work in the building and nobody's seen before."

Jim sat puzzled. "Why?"

"Because fired people get pissed off. Some even start shooting. I'm sure you've seen the headlines." The executive came around and sat casually against the front corner of his desk. "Who needs that kind of shit in their lives?"

"So I'm getting paid to have people shoot at me?"

The executive waved dismissively and walked back around his desk. "Probably never happen. Most of the shooters have to go home to get their guns. By the time they get back, you'll at least be able to make it to the parking lot, maybe the highway, if you're lucky."

"Sounds dangerous, especially if they realize I know nothing about their business and have no legitimate basis to fire them."

"Oh, they'll definitely realize that. It's part of the plan."

"Plan?"

"Most of the firings are unjust anyway, merely to dazzle Wall Street by cutting operating costs in the portfolio and making top management rich from stock options. So if these employees are given walking papers by some consultant who wouldn't last a day in their mail room, it shifts blame for the injustice—and the direction of the gun barrel."

"But why me?"

"Because you're non-confrontational." The executive opened a file and removed a computer scan sheet with little ovals filled in with a number-two pencil. "The psychological test when you applied." He leaned back in his desk chair and held the sheet toward a ceiling light. "In all our years, we've never seen anyone score so high in conflict avoidance."

"I don't think I agree with what this company—"

"You're wrong!"

"Okay . . ."

"That's the spirit."

So Jim hopscotched from Clearwater to St. Petersburg to Sarasota, firing people and apologizing that it was the wrong thing to do. Then the economy picked up, and the demand to fire people dropped, so his consulting company hired another consulting company, which fired Jim.

A decade passed. The economy tanked again. Jim was back in business.

On this particular day in December, Jim took Interstate 4 out to a distribution warehouse in Lakeland, just east of Tampa.

The company gave Jim a temporary office close to the parking lot.

A knock on the door.

Jim waved the person in through the glass. The employee stuck his head inside. "They told me to see you?"

Jim gestured with an upturned palm. "Have a seat." He faced the employee with an expression like his dog had died. "I'm afraid I have some bad news . . ."

Five minutes later:

"You're firing me a week before Christmas!"

"I know." Jim looked down at the desk. "It's very wrong."

"You don't know shit about this business, do you?"

"Not really."

"Then how is this fair?"

"It's not."

"I'll bet your name isn't even Jensen Beach. They're keeping your actual name a secret to protect you from retaliation."

"You're right."

"Well, I'm going to find out what it really is!" The employee got up and went to the door. "How do you sleep at night, motherfucker?"

The door slammed.

Jim hopped up, grabbed his briefcase, and walked swiftly to where a security guard was holding open a side door to the parking lot. "We moved your car closer. Hurry . . ."

Jim half walked, half trotted to his car. He stuck a key in the door.

From behind: "There you are!"

Jim spun around . . .

Spreading misery day in, day out wasn't Jim's cup of tea, money or not. He would have quit long ago, except he received a second set of duties. Because all the firings were simply window dressing to impress Wall Street, many of the companies became severely understaffed and unable to meet quarterly projections. Wall Street wasn't impressed.

His consulting company needed headhunters. They called Jim in. He knew just where to look for new employees: the totally qualified old ones he had just fired.

His bosses were bowled over. "Where are you finding all these great prospects? Our clients are thrilled!"

They gave him a promotion and a company car.

It was the same car that Jim now stood next to in the parking lot of a Lakeland distribution warehouse as a husky man charged toward him. Jim hurried with the keys, but his hands were shaking too badly. The man reached Jim and seized him with both arms in a bear hug, lifting him off the ground.

"Oh, thank you! Thank you! Thank you! I haven't been able to find a job in months, and now I get one just before Christmas! My children will have presents! It's all because of you!"

With all the firing and hiring, there wasn't much middle emotional ground in Jim's line. All mountain peaks and mine shafts. On average, his work mood was indifferent. He was very happy.

But that was Jim. Counting his blessings. And over-thinking the worst-case scenario.

As the man had asked, how did he sleep at night? Two eyes open, staring at the ceiling. Then the digital alarm clock with green numbers: 2:04, 2:44, 3:19. Perspiration. Aware of every heartbeat. Running checklists of family precautions through his mind. To look at Jim was, well, to look at anyone else on the street. Non-muscular, a little on the thin side. The kind of person people can't identify to police. "He was just average." "Anything else?" "Seemed the quiet type, like he could be pushed around."

Martha Davenport took up the slack. Attractive in a mature way. Which meant unpretentious clothing that hid the fact she was even more attractive. And full-bodied, fiery red hair that didn't lie about her temperament. She slept the sleep of small children.

In one way, Jim was like Spock from *Star Trek*, calmly computing any conflict through to all permutations of final outcome, deciding that most were pointless and perilous enough to be strenuously avoided. Martha started at DEFCON 5 and went from there. She had opposed Melvin playing Little League, because of how she heard the other parents behaved. Then, clinging the chain-link fence behind home plate: "Ump! Are you blind?"

In their case, however, the extremes of the marriage created a whole that was greater than the sum of the parts. All in all, a good collaboration, like Lennon-McCartney.

A company car finished the drive back from Lakeland and pulled up a driveway on Triggerfish Lane. Jim came through the front door with his briefcase. "Honey, I'm home . . ."

"How was your day?" asked Martha.

"Great!" said Jim, loosening his tie. "It was so-so."

"I had a great day, too," said Martha. "I went to the mall."

"Find something on sale?"

"No, I went to see the assistant manager about that mall cop."

"I thought you handled that on the phone."

Martha shook her head. "They called back. Said they couldn't prove anything about the fight in the bathroom, and they reviewed the security tapes. Concluded it was elves after all. So they wanted to interview me."

Jim folded his jacket over the back of a chair. "What for?"

"Said they wanted to fire him anyway, and needed more details about my complaint."

"Honey, I really wish you hadn't done that."

"Why?" said Martha. "I'm tired of the jerks getting away with stuff. It seems people like us who obey the rules are the only ones who ever get punished."

She grabbed a pair of binoculars from a drawer.

"What are you doing?"

Martha walked to the window. "We're getting new neighbors. That rental house across the street. I saw the landlord take down the sign and change the locks today."

"I'm not sure you should be looking out our front window with binoculars."

"Relax, everyone on the street does it." She adjusted the focus. "I wonder what we'll get this time. Hope they're like those nice Flanagans whose kids used to babysit Nicole when she was younger. Hope it's not like the Raifords, whose dogs kept getting loose . . . ."

"And who received a copy of your anonymous dog complaint."

"They were the ones breaking the rules. And then they blamed us, making crank calls at all hours."

"I remember that," said Jim. "Using pay phones so the calls couldn't be traced when you reported it to the police."

Martha scanned the windows, trying to see if any furniture had arrived. "Remember the dental hygienist who left the blinds open and had men coming and going, and that old man who kept digging holes in his yard in the middle of the night? . . ."

"The police never found anything after you called."

" . . . The newlyweds who never left the house for weeks until all his clothes were on fire in the driveway, and those college kids who left the door open and played Pink Floyd all the time, and . . . Oh no." Martha slowly lowered the binoculars.

"What is it?" asked Jim. "Jesus, those veins in your head are throbbing again."

Across the street, a '72 Chevelle pulled up. The driver's door opened. "Coleman, imagine our luck being able to rent a house so close to the Davenports. I can't wait to see the look on their faces!"

CHAPTER SIX

THE NEXT MORNING

Birds chirped.

More accurately squawked. Green parrots. Flying over the light poles in the parking lot of the new Tampa Bay Mall.

The stores hadn't opened yet. Just janitors and power walkers with hand weights. Security bars began cranking up in front of the Cutlery Castle. Someone else turned on a stove at the Magic Wok.

A mall cop strolled along the second level, past one of the power walkers who got a little ambitious.

"No running!" said the security guard. A corridor approached. The guard walked past the restrooms and knocked on the last door. He stuck his head inside. "You wanted to see me?"

"Come in and have a seat," said the assistant mall manager. Serious mouth. Holding a report in his hands.

Five minutes later. "Son of a bitch!"

"We can't have personnel yelling at children, and especially not mothers. They're our best customers."

"What's her name?" The guard lunged from his chair with an outstretched arm. "Let me see that fucking complaint!"

The assistant manager yanked the complaint out of reach high over his head. "It's anonymous."

The ex-mall cop stood. "I'm going to find out who reported me if it's the last thing I do!"

He flung the office door open. Someone was waiting in the hall; that person jumped out of the way as the fired guard stormed past.

The assistant mall manager slipped the complaint in the top drawer of his desk, then smiled and waved for the person waiting in the hall to enter the office. "Come in, come in, Mr. Beach. Corporate told me you'd be here."

"Please call me Jensen," said Jim Davenport.

"Okay, Jensen, pull up a chair." The assistant manager took a seat behind his desk and leaned forward on elbows. "Now, what can I do for you?"

"I'm sure you know that retail is in a slump."

The manager leaned back in his chair with fingers interlaced behind his head. "Yeah, everyone's a little off. Sausage World pulled out last month. But it all goes in cycles; everyone bounces back."

"I'm happy to hear you see it that way." Jim opened his briefcase on his lap. "That'll make this go a lot easier."

"What do you mean by that? . . ."

Five minutes later:

"Motherfucker! You're firing *me*? Do you know anything at all about mall administration?"

"Not remotely."

"So you have no real basis to fire me instead of one of the other assistant managers."

"Not that I can think of."

"What about Johnson? He hasn't been here half as long as me. It isn't fair!"

"You're right," said Jim. "It's not."

"Get out of my office."

"Actually they said you had to leave . . ."

"I'm not going anywhere."

" . . . And if you said you weren't going anywhere, I was instructed to call mall security."

"We've got one guy working today," said the assistant manager. "And he isn't working here anymore—"

A cell phone rang. Jim held up a finger to wait a second. He recognized the numerical display as the number of his supervisor at Sunshine Solutions. "Hello? . . . Yes, actually I'm here right now . . . Another hiring job? . . . They're short-staffed? . . . But why do they need to fill the position so fast? . . . An urgent human resources problem has come up? . . . I'll get right on it."

Jim closed the phone.

The manager was standing. "Now, are you going to leave by yourself, or will I have to kick your ass?"

"No, I'm going," said Jim. He picked up his briefcase and left the office, looking to hire a security guard to remove the assistant manager from the building.

The front curtains parted a slit.

Binoculars poked through. "Jim, come here," said Martha.

Jim drilled a wall anchor to hang the newest Davenport family portrait taken at Just Portraits. "What is it?"

"They're back."

Jim walked across the living room. "Martha, are you going to spend your whole life at the window?"

"They've got a bunch of stuff in the trunk."

"That's a mystery. People moving in, having stuff."

"Don't trivialize me." She opened the curtains wider. "Those men are dangerous. I wonder what's in all those bags? . . ."

Across the street, Coleman hoisted a sack out of the trunk. "What's in all these bags?"

"Christmas!" said Serge, grabbing his own bag. "This is going to be the best ever!"

They headed for the front door.

Coleman set his bag down and leaned against the house. "I'm tired."

Serge got out his keys. "You only walked from the driveway to the porch."

"Maybe it's the marijuana."

"Gee, you think?" They went inside and Serge dumped the bags' contents on the floor. Then five more trips to the car until the pile in the living room was a mountain.

"Why so much shit?" asked Coleman.

"Because I love Christmas! But usually I'm too busy

with all my business travel and outstanding warrants. Not this year! My new motto: 'I'm taking Christmas big!'" Serge dropped to his knees and pawed through the mound on the floor. "Here's the plan: We do everything, all the traditions, and we do it grander than anyone ever dreamed! Here are the houselights, which will require extra generators so we don't smash the power grid, the holiday music CDs that will need weatherproof outdoor concert speakers, the train set with extra boxes of tracks to connect all the rooms of the house, the bicycle whose assembly on Christmas Eve will make us use profanity like Kid Rock, the toys where we forget the batteries, several gingerbread house kits we'll combine to form a mansion, DVDs of all the classic Christmas specials to run nonstop, mistletoe for all the doorways, the manger scene with a little Jesus that glows in the dark to emphasize the Holy Spirit third of the Trinity because he's the shy one who gets the least press, all the presents we'll wrap together and give each other as Secret Santas . . ."

Coleman popped a special holiday-edition Budweiser. "But if we wrap the presents together, I'll already know what you bought me."

Serge untangled a strand of lights. "You won't remember."

Coleman took a gulp from his beer. "I love surprises."

Serge jumped up. "Let's get the tree! . . ."

Across the street: "Look at the size of that tree tied to the roof of their Chevelle," said Martha. "It's almost as long as the car."

"I don't think they'll be able to get it in the house," said Jim.

Moments later: "Push!" yelled Serge.

"I'm pushing as hard as I can," said Coleman. "The door's not big enough."

"Then we'll figure something else out . . . Pull!"

"I'm pulling as hard as I can. I think it's stuck."

"Let me get out there and help." Serge crouched on his hands and knees and crawled through the front door under the tree. He stood up next to Coleman. "Get a good grip and pull as hard as you can on three . . . Three!"

Grunting and more grunting.

"It's stuck good," said Coleman.

Serge let go. "Fuck it. Leave it there. Can't let this slow down the yuletide juggernaut."

They crawled under the tree and into the house. Coleman grabbed another cold one. "Why was it so important to rent a house near Jim's place, anyway?"

"Because he's my hero." Serge began nailing stockings to the wall. "The courage of holding down a family. I want to be just like him, and what better way than to live as close as possible and observe his secrets? We'll tap into their rhythms and mimic everything they do until it becomes natural."

"What's the point?"

"I'm taking it to the next level!" Serge grabbed a nail from his teeth and resumed hammering. "Don't get me wrong. Fleeing all over the state from the cops, staying in crappy motels, and stealing shit has its place. But you need to raise a family to grow as a human. And what better time to start than Christmas?"

"But we're not a family," said Coleman.

"But we are!" said Serge. He went to the dining table. "Just need to get some chicks in the mix, and the whole family dynamic will take care of itself."

"Who are you thinking of?"

Serge just smiled.

Coleman took a step back. "You don't mean . . ."

"That's right. City and Country!"

Coleman took an extra-long guzzle from a bottle of Jack to steady his nerves. "Those are some badass babes. But they're still on the run for that murder."

"Except they didn't do it. They're innocent."

"Maybe they were innocent back then, but all the years on the lam. Who knows how many crimes?"

Serge began tapping on the laptop. "We're judging?"

"No. I wouldn't mind seeing them again. They're smokin' hot!" Coleman took a slug of whiskey and cracked open two beers. "But they're in deep hiding. How are you going to find them?"

"How all fugitives keep in touch. Facebook." Serge typed a few more minutes. "There, found them. Now I'll just send our new address, then poke them and hit them with snowballs for good measure . . . They'll be here in no time."

Serge closed the laptop and walked to the front window.

Coleman followed, snorting off the back of his hand.

"Is that cocaine?" asked Serge.

Coleman's eye sparkled. "White Christmas, dude!" He leaned in for another snort. "What do we do until the babes get here?"

"Study the Davenports' lifestyle so we'll know how to start a family. Of course we'll have to invade their privacy, but it's what everyone does in the suburbs. I didn't make the rules." He raised a pair of binoculars and aimed them across the street, where he saw Martha staring back at him with her own binoculars.

Serge smiled and waved.

TAMPA BAY MALL

One of the assistant managers barricaded himself in his office, but nobody had noticed yet.

A mall cop arrived.

Not the new recruit Jim Davenport had just hired.

He pounded on the door. "Give me that anonymous complaint!"

"No!"

"I want it now!"

"Go away!"

"I'll kick the door in!"

"I've got a gun!"

"You do not!" The fired security guard began crashing into the door with his shoulder until it finally gave and splintered off the hinges.

The guard ran to the front of the desk. "Give me that complaint!"

The assistant manager took up a defensive position on the other side. "I don't have it!"

"It's in that top drawer, isn't it?"

"No." The manager opened the drawer and grabbed it.

The guard faked left and right on the front of the desk. "Give it to me."

The manager countered, right and left. "Stay away from me!"

"Then I'll chase you!"

"You can't catch me!"

"Right!" The guard took off around one end of the desk. The manager ran around the other. Circle after circle.

"Give it to me!"

"Can't have it!"

The guard closed in, right on the manager's heels. He reached and snatched. But missed the complaint.

"Hey! My toupee!"

"Give me the complaint!"

"Not a chance."

"Fine." The guard took out a cigarette lighter and set the hairpiece on fire. "See what you get?" He dropped the still-burning rug in the wastebasket.

The bald man used the opportunity to make a break for the door. He turned the knob and opened it a half foot before the guard caught him from behind and slammed it shut.

The manager crumpled the page into a ball.

"Give it to me!"

"Mmmm-mmmm!"

"You better not be sticking that in your mouth!"

"Mmmm-mmmm!"

The guard spun him around and punched him in the stomach.

"Ahhhh!"

A ball of paper flew across the room. The guard ran

after it. The manager tackled him from behind and twisted his ankle. The guard kicked him in the face. The burning toupee set off the sprinkler system. "Let go of my leg!"

Another twist, another kick. "Ow! Ow!"

The guard dragged the manager until he finally reached the ball of paper.

The bald assistant manager let go and reached in the trash can. He held up something that looked like roadkill. Tears began to roll.

The guard sat up on the ground and uncrumpled the page. "Martha Davenport . . . But where's the address? Trigger-something. Shoot, it's smeared too much from the sprinklers . . . Hold everything. Davenport, Davenport. Where have I heard that name before?" The guard suddenly snapped his fingers. "I got it. Those elves! This Davenport woman got me fired *and* beat up. Well, I better destroy this report so nobody can trace it back to me after I exact my revenge—"

An ax came through the door. Then two firefighters. They looked down at an assistant mall manager crying and wearing a melted toupee, sitting cross-legged next to a mall cop with a bleeding ankle and a mouth full of paper.

One of the firefighters looked at the other. "Not again."

CHAPTER SEVEN

TRIGGERFISH LANE

Serge spied out the front window with binoculars.

Coleman wiggled a pop-top off a beer can. "What's going on?"

Serge panned the house across the street. "Martha's staring at me with binoculars and Jim is decorating the tree. That's our cue."

"For what?"

"Decorate our tree. We've got to copy exactly everything he does or the plan could fail." Serge headed for the kitchen. "I'll get the popcorn going and grab the sewing kit."

"Get some sewing stuff for me, too."

The scene became industrious. Perry Como on TV.

Serge came through the dining room and glanced at the table. "Coleman, you already built the gingerbread house— I mean mansion."

"I was motivated to accomplish something."

"I can't process that sentence."

"Dig!" said Coleman.

Serge squatted down with his chin on the edge of the table, admiring the handiwork. "How come all the windows are shuttered closed?"

"That's a surprise."

More holiday preparation bustle.

Coleman ended up seated at the kitchen table with needle and thread. Serge dumped a brown bag on the table and took a chair on the other side.

Coleman hit a joint and resumed a rare spasm of work. "What's all that junk?"

Serge grabbed scissors and cut his own length of thread. "Any Christmas of mine must have a Florida theme. So I rounded up some ornamental fodder: matchbooks, bar coasters, ashtrays, pins, buttons, parking tickets, plastic cups from sporting events, swizzle sticks, cocktail umbrellas . . ." Serge squinted with one eye closed and threaded a needle through a piece of popcorn. ". . . rubber alligators and sharks from roadside attractions, souvenir butane lighters, keepsake bottle openers, Welcome-to-Florida matching penis and boobs salt-and-pepper shakers . . ."

Coleman squinted with his own thread. "What's going to be the angel for the top of the tree?"

"That's the best part!" Serge pulled something from another bag next to his chair. "Isn't it great?"

Coleman scratched his head. "It's just a little toy gorilla."

"Bought it at Toy Town."

"But what's that got to do with Florida?"

"They didn't have what I really wanted, so I had to settle for this and perform custom alterations." Serge tapped the gorilla's chest.

Coleman edged closer. "You just wrapped masking tape a bunch of times around its chest and used a Magic Marker to write 'Everglades Skunk Ape.'"

Serge set the gorilla down and grabbed a piece of popcorn. "Bet I've got the only one."

Twenty minutes later, they finished at the table. Serge jumped to his feet. "To the tree!"

More activity fastening things that weren't meant to be fastened to the tree's branches.

Coleman worked with a stapler. *Click-click, click-click.* "Serge? When are we going to put the tree where it's finally going to go?"

Serge used a crimping tool for heavy-gauge industrial wire. *Ker-chunk, ker-chunk.* "It's already in the final place."

Coleman stapled theme-park tickets. "But it's still stuck in the door."

"It's way too damn big to get inside. I don't know what I was thinking." Serge hung a snow globe of dolphins on a teeter-totter. "So I figured we'd just leave it here and share the joy with our new neighbors."

"It's sticking out horizontal. I've never seen a sideways Christmas tree before."

"And neither has the neighborhood decorating committee. We might win a ribbon." Serge grabbed a roll of duct tape. "Damn, my skunk ape keeps drooping over . . ."

"Nice popcorn garland," said Coleman.

"Then stop eating it."

"But I'm hungry."

"I'm impressed by your garland, too," said Serge. "Cool strands of beer-can pop-tops."

"Thanks."

Serge held one of the lengths. "What are these little clear plastic squares in between?"

"Crack-cocaine baggies I found in alleys."

"Good Florida touch. And this ornament?"

"I made it with a nail file."

"Candy-cane shiv? . . ."

A squeal of tires. Serge and Coleman looked up. A GTX with gold rims parked at the Davenports' curb. Necking.

Serge stood. "Hold down the Christmas fort. I need to take care of something." He trotted toward the street.

The door of the Davenport residence opened. Martha came down the steps.

Serge reached the driver's side and knocked on the glass. The window rolled down halfway. "What the fuck do you want?"

"Excuse me, Mr. Snake, but if you'd like to hit it off with a girl's parents, it's usually better to go up and introduce yourself than to sit in the street molesting their fifteen-year-old in full view of the neighborhood. I'm just taking a wild stab at this."

"Eat shit and die, old man."

The GTX patched out. Serge was left standing in the middle of the road . . . staring at Martha, who'd just arrived on the other side before the car sped off.

Serge smiled awkwardly. "Do I look old?"

Martha gritted her teeth. "You!"

Serge placed a hand over his heart with innocent surprise. "Me?" Then pointed down the road with the other arm. "It's Mr. Snake who was tongue-wrestling your daughter. Not to mention whatever was going on below window level that we couldn't see. I remember when I was his age." Serge chuckled to himself and shook his head. "They called it 'necking.' No kidding. I just couldn't seem to keep my neck in my pants. Ah, fond memories . . ." He paused to study Martha's red-faced expression. "Why don't you like me?"

Her nostrils flared. "If you don't—!"

Crash.

They both looked over at Serge's rental house, where a rusted-out Pinto had just slammed into the garbage cans down at the curb. Two women got out. Any man on the street who had heard the crash was now glued to his window staring at the twin sites: statuesque, hot, fatal, looking like they'd gotten dressed in the *Dukes of Hazzard* wardrobe trailer. The blonde had a bottle of Jim Beam by the neck, and the brunette threw the stub of a small Clint Eastwood cigar in the street.

Serge grinned at Martha and jerked a thumb over his shoulder. "Got to run. The chicks are here . . . Guess what? We're starting a family!" He took off running. "We're going to be just like you!"

Jim came down to the street and joined his wife at the curb. "I heard a crash. What's going on?"

"I'm going to kill him!"

"Who are those women?"

Martha just stared in simmering fury.

Across the street, the women headed up the walkway toward the house. Serge ran to meet them halfway. Coleman came down from the porch.

"City! Country!" said Serge. "Long time no see—"

The blonde spun and caught him in the jaw with a sledgehammer right cross, decking him soundly. The brunette twirled with a roundhouse kung fu kick that whipped Coleman in the back of the calves and knocked his legs out from under him.

Jim watched as two men moaned in pain, rolling on the lawn across the street. Two women passed a bottle of whiskey. "Martha, what's going on?"

"He said they're starting a family."

MEANWHILE. . .

In a modest subdivision on Tampa's east side, a bald man sat inside his three-bedroom cookie-cutter ranch house with screened-in swimming pool.

He was on the phone. On hold. Melted toupee in the trash can.

A woman finally answered. The man sat up straight. "Hello, this is Phil Westwood from the Tampa Bay Mall, and I'd like to speak to one of your consultants, Jensen Beach . . . I see, unavailable . . . Would you have a cell number or personal mailing address? . . . No, I understand completely that you can't give out that kind of information. It's just that he recently performed some terrific work for the mall, and I'd like to give him a present to show our appreciation . . . Send it to your company? I'd sort of like it to be more personal . . . You can deliver a personal message to him at his desk right now? But I thought you said he was out . . . Oh, you said *unavailable* . . . Yes, in his line of work you have to protect him from kooks. Never know when one of those would call. Thanks for your time."

He hung up. "Damn."

Then he swiveled back to his computer and stared at the screen, where he had just looked up the phone number for Sunshine Solutions—and had no luck at all with a Mr. Jensen Beach. "Think! Think! . . ." He tapped fingers on top of his shiny dome, then back to the keyboard. "If I can't find that consultant, then I want to know who that woman is." He glanced at the wastebasket. "Her stupid freaking complaint!"

His wife appeared in the den's doorway. "Honey, your dinner's getting cold."

"I'm busy."

"I feel so badly for you, but it might be good to get your mind off it." She pursed her lips with genuine concern. "It's been two days now."

"Get my mind off it? I was fired and beat up within twenty-four hours." He continued typing on the keyboard. "Neither has happened in fifteen years, and one not since grade school."

She went to say something, then stopped and left the room to put something back in the oven.

More typing. "Here we go, Facebook. Martha Davenport . . . Bingo! That's her all right. Wish I still had that stupid report. The address was right in my fingers . . . Wait, what's this family photo? Her husband looks familiar. But where have I seen . . . Oh my God. Jensen Beach is her husband, Jim. The Davenports are responsible for both my beating and my firing!" He quickly surfed back to the local phone directory and scribbled something on a pad. "Okay, calm down and take this slow. See where this asshole lives and get the lay of the land. Then figure out a plan."

He snatched keys off the desk.

His wife was back in the doorway. She turned as he went by. "Are you going to eat at all tonight?"

"I don't know." And out the front door.

The ex-assistant mall manager climbed in a brown Ford Focus station wagon and headed east, passing a convenience store with two Ram pickup trucks parked side by side. Both had parking stickers for a distribution warehouse in Lakeland. An arm came out one of the windows, passing a sheet of paper to someone in the other.

"Appreciate it, Jerry."

"It's so unfair you were fired."

The second man read the page. "So his real name's Jim Davenport, Triggerfish Lane." He looked up. "How'd you get this?"

"You don't want to know. But can you do me a favor? Nothing too extreme."

"Don't worry—"

"No, really. I can imagine how I'd react, and I don't want you to make me an accessory."

They were about to pull out, when the lead pickup was cut off by a black Delta 88 with an ex-mall cop behind the wheel. On the passenger seat, a formerly soggy anonymous complaint was now flattened out and crisp from meticulous work with a hair dryer. Beside it, a map of Tampa and a handwritten list of possible address matches to the partial ID on the complaint.

The Delta 88 took a ramp for the Crosstown Expressway, hitting the tollbooth a minute between a Ford Focus and a Ram pickup.

TRIGGERFISH LANE

Serge stood up in the middle of the lawn, rubbing his jaw. "Have to admit, you still got it."

"You son of a bitch!" yelled the blonde. "You did it to us again."

Coleman stood up more slowly, and the brunette kicked him in the crotch. "You left us stranded on the side of the road. That's three times. And after all we put up with, living in all those douche-bag motels!"

Serge spread his arms. "This time will be different! I swear!"

"Bullshit!" said the blonde.

"No, really," said Serge. "We now have an actual home in a nice neighborhood."

"What's the scam this time?" asked the brunette.

"Why do you always think there's a scam with me?"

"Because there always is."

"Except this time will be different from all the others. We're going to form a solid family unit, live the American Dream and greet census takers and everything."

The women exchanged dubious looks.

Other neighbors tentatively wandered out into their yards to snoop.

The blonde turned back to Serge. "First, a family isn't made of two couples. Second, only one of us is a couple, and not even that. You and I just screw when we're horny."

"Many relationships have been built on that," said Serge. "Actually, I'm thinking most."

The brunette pointed demonstratively at Coleman. "I am not fucking that man!"

Neighbors nonchalantly edged closer to their sidewalks.

"But, Serge," said the blonde. "What gave you such a crackpot idea in the first place?"

Serge turned with fully outstretched arms. "We're going to be just like them!"

The women looked to see the Davenports staring back from the other side of the street, Martha giving them the stink eye.

The blonde took a step forward. "What are you looking at, bitch?"

"Bitch?" yelled Martha. "Why, you cunt!"

Jim shrieked and jumped in front of Martha. "Let's go back in the house . . ."

Serge grabbed the blonde around the waist from behind. "Easy there, girl. You can't give her a beat-down. The other neighbors won't invite you to tea."

Martha snarled as Jim led her away.

The blonde glared back as Serge steered her toward the house. "Let's all go inside. I'll bet you're itching to see the new place!"

"I got some killer red bud," said Coleman.

"I guess it wouldn't hurt to take a peek around," said the blonde.

"There's a Christmas tree stuck sideways in the door," said the brunette.

"We're trying to win a ribbon," said Serge.

The foursome got on their hands and knees and started crawling under the tree.

"Hold it," said Coleman, standing back up. "There's some cards in the mailbox . . . Do we know anybody from Christmas, Florida?"

CHAPTER EIGHT

ONE HOUR LATER

Dining room table.

Coleman and the two women sat around the gingerbread house.

The blonde had her mouth over the chimney.

Coleman flicked a Bic lighter and held it to a tiny flowerpot near the front door.

A watery, bubbling sound.

Serge stood in the background, scratching his head with a puzzled expression. "Coleman, what kind of weirdness am I looking at here?"

"It's a bong."

"That was your motivation?"

Coleman flicked the lighter again. "No other point to put myself through that kind of work."

"Silly me," said Serge. "But it's going to make the gingerbread taste awful. We'll have to throw it out."

"Like hell," said Coleman. "I baked pot into the walls, and the frosting."

"Nice work, Hansel." Serge turned. "So, ladies, I've been meaning to ask. What names are you going by these days?"

The brunette exhaled a hit from the chimney. "She's Crystal River and I'm Belle Glade."

"Nice ring," said Serge. "Almost as good as City and Country . . ."

City and Country, products of their environment. Tuscaloosa, Alabama, to put a pin in the map. Town girls in a university town. Hardworking, no drugs or wild weekends, not the remotest legal scrape between them. Until the night they went in that student bar. Some coked-out sorority sister fell on the knife she'd been using to cut rails in a toilet stall. The girls found her. Pulled out the blade, tried mouth-to-mouth. It stacked up fast. Fingerprints, blood, victim's father a huge donor to the law school. They didn't stick around for the opinion polls; on the run ever since, which just hit the ten-year mark. Couldn't stay in one place long, couldn't give Social Security numbers. Their employers knew the score and took advantage. Waitress gigs, saloons, strip clubs. It was a hard decade, and they came out the back end as hard as they make 'em. Country had grown up on remote farmland a half hour toward Muscle Shoals. City was a transplant from the Bronx. To cast the movie, you might pick Daryl Hannah and Halle Berry.

"Coleman," said Country. "What the hell's Serge doing?"

Coleman glanced over his shoulder. "Looking out the window with binoculars to see how Jim does it."

"Does what?"

Coleman shrugged.

"There seems to be a lot of traffic on the street," said Serge, swinging the binoculars left to right. "A minute ago, a Ford Focus went by, then a Delta 88, and now a Ram pickup."

"Why is that unusual?" asked Coleman.

"It's the second or third time I've seen each, and they're all slowing down in front of Jim's house like they're looking for an address or something . . . Now Martha's coming out of the house. She's screaming at Jim, who's standing bewildered in the doorway. Looks like he's in shit. Now he's making desperate gestures to explain, which means he's only making the shit deeper. That's the key to love: Never explain yourself. If a woman attacks, and your response is explanations, then strap on a helmet. But that's just my experience. I'm sure Jim knows what he's doing. And this is the perfect chance!"

"What chance?" asked Coleman.

"Martha just fishtailed out of the driveway and hit our garbage cans speeding away. That means it's bachelor night for lucky Jim! We'll get him over here to pick his brain and learn his secrets . . . Be right back." Serge tossed the binoculars on the sofa and crawled under the Christmas tree.

Across the street: *Ding-dong . . . Ding-dong . . . Ding-dong. . .*

Jim ran and opened the door. "Jesus, Serge, how many times are you going to ring the doorbell?"

Ding-dong . . . "That's the last one. So listen, Martha's seriously fucking pissed at you, so come on over and have laughs."

"No! In fact . . ." Jim stuck his head outside and looked both ways. "You need to get out of here before Martha sees you. She could be back any minute."

Serge shook his head. "Not the way she almost clipped that stop sign at the end of the street. You've got two solid hours minimum."

"Serge," said Jim. "There's absolutely no way on earth I'm going over there—"

Fleet, quiet footsteps across the lawn. Serge looked back. "Country, what brings you to this pleasant abode? Decided to help me invite Jim into joining us?"

She bounded up the porch steps. "I want to break some of her shit! Calling me a cunt!"

Serge braced himself in the doorway with both arms. "You're not breaking anything."

Country tried to force her way past. "I'll bet she loves that china cabinet."

"Not the china cabinet!" said Jim.

Serge made a guttural straining sound. "Don't think I can hold her much longer. But if you give me a hand, we might be able to get her back across the street and calm her down. Otherwise, you might want to check your home owner's deductible."

"Darn it, okay, if that's what it takes. Her grandmother gave her that cabinet." Jim grabbed his house keys. "But I can't stay."

"Now you're talking," said Serge. "You won't regret . . ."

Coleman and City were still at the dining room table when three people crawled under the Christmas tree.

Serge bounced up. "Hey everyone, it's Jim!"

"Yo, Jimbo," said Coleman, saluting with a joint. "What's up?"

Serge helped Jim to his feet. "He's going to share all his secrets on holding a family together and making the nation secure. And maybe, just maybe shrink our carbon footprint."

"No, no, no!" said Jim. "I just came to get her home. Like we agreed."

"Okay, the footprint was just wishful thinking." Serge clasped his hands together. "Then let's not waste any of Jim's time! Coleman, chair!"

Coleman kicked one out for Jim to take a seat at the table.

"I can't sit, Serge! I have to go."

"Look out for the train," said Serge.

"What train?"

A little locomotive whistle blew, and a model train came around the bend from the kitchen, toward Jim's feet. He hopped back out of the way and fell into the chair.

"That's better," said Serge.

The train circled the table and disappeared into one of the bedrooms. City passed the joint to Jim, who waved her off without words. Country took a swig of whiskey from the bottle and grabbed the roach.

Jim started getting up. Country pushed him back down and handed him the bottle—"Ease out. Your stress is a buzz kill"—headed for the kitchen and more ice.

Jim tried passing the bottle toward Serge, who pulled back his hands. "You're on your own with these women. I'm sure your techniques are rock solid, but these are the chicks I'll be dealing with, so I need to see if your interaction with them passes the acid test."

Jim turned and handed the bottle toward Coleman.

"My hands are busy." Coleman broke down the walls of the gingerbread house.

Country came back with clean glasses and ice. "Jim, here's yours."

"But I rarely drink." He turned toward Serge.

"Don't look at me. Acid test."

Jim looked back up at Country and held a thumb and index finger a quarter inch apart. "Okay, but just a little."

She poured four fingers and splashed a fifth on the table, then jammed the rocks glass in Jim's stomach and wandered away, upending the bottle.

"Feet," said Serge.

Jim looked down and swiftly raised them. The Orange Blossom Special rolled under his chair and chugged out of sight into the bathroom.

"So, Jim," said Serge. "What's your first tip to someone starting a family? Begin with the biggest thing!"

"Actually the biggest thing is the smallest thing."

"Jim," said Serge. "You're talking Zen warrior shaman shit. Is the Eastern jazz what it's all about?"

"No, I mean that the little things are what make your wife happy and your marriage solid, because after a while it isn't fairy-tale royals' weddings; it's commitment to each other's small considerations during the marathon of raising children."

"Example?" said Serge.

"Not tracking stuff into the house."

Serge's head jerked back. "You're blowin' smoke up my ass. *That's* number one?"

"Not the least speck of dirt. They spend so much time vacuuming and mopping." Jim raised the glass to his mouth for a sip. More like sticking in the tip of his tongue for a taste. He made a face. "It shows you appreciate her efforts."

City took a big hit—"He's on the money"—then blew Country a sensuous shotgun that gave all the guys boners.

Country exhaled. "Don't wipe your shoes, no pussy."

"Jim," said Serge. "You're in the zone! Dr. Phil can't carry your jockstrap. What else?"

Jim raised the glass for another tongue test. Verdict: not bad. He took a moderate sip. Then another. Then he finished the drink. A look on his face. He began coughing and slapping his chest.

"You all right?" asked Serge. "Go down the wrong way?"

"No, just burns." His eyes bugged and watered.

"Whiskey does that," said Serge.

Jim looked at his watch. "What time is it? I need to be getting back."

"I don't think that's a good idea right now," said Serge. "Just sit still a moment and gather yourself." He offered a tissue. "You got a little spit coming off . . ."

Quiet around the table except for an unending series of watery bubbling episodes. Finally: "I'm better now." Jim whistled. "But I'm really feeling that drink. Where was I?"

"Wiping feet."

"Uh, yeah. When I mentioned not tracking stuff in, that really isn't number one."

"You must tell," said Serge. "The knowledge that is the source of all truth . . ." He got up and bent into a Karate Kid pose.

"Number one is actually peeing."

"Hold that thought." Serge stuck a finger in his ear and wiggled it around. "Must have wax buildup. I thought I heard you say peeing."

"I did," said Jim. "There are all kinds of guidebooks to educate the genders about each other's sexual physiology. But the real ignorance zone is how we urinate."

"Jim," asked Serge, "are you on some kind of medication where you're not allowed to drink alcohol?"

"Hear me out. You ever wander into the ladies' room by mistake, like at a restaurant?"

"Who hasn't?"

"What did you notice?"

"It was clean," said Serge. "Like an operating room."

"And men's restrooms?"

"A disgrace," said Serge. "Especially when it's a busy place like a sports arena, and all the urinals are taken and they have to use the toilets to pee. Might as well set a pack of chimpanzees loose in there."

"Exactly," said Jim. "Men were built for urinals, not toilets. But homes only have toilets. Even the most careful guy can't prevent a certain amount of sprinkle and ambient mist, not to mention a little splashing from the bowl if your stream's strong enough."

"I follow," said Serge. "Women don't realize we really are trying as hard as we can, but it's a curse. They think we're not aiming at all." Serge looked across the table. "Country?"

She raised her mouth from the chimney. "You *aren't* aiming. You just go in hosing wherever you like."

"Yeah," said City. "We're tired of cleaning that nastiness up."

Serge looked back at Jim. "Pray tell, what can we possibly do? We're only men."

"If you really love a woman," said Jim, "then right at the beginning of the relationship, you have to get your arms around the urine issue. After every use, wipe the place down like you're leaving a crime scene because, in a way, you are."

"Brilliant!" said Serge. "Any other gems? Like earlier when I saw Martha outside yelling like a banshee, and you were trying to explain yourself. Explaining goes against everything I've ever heard, centuries of men comparing notes. Have you made some kind of breakthrough that hasn't hit the news yet?"

"No." Jim looked down at the table. "Trying to explain was a mistake. It's the toilet thing again."

Serge sat back in surprise. "But after all you just said. I thought you were the master."

"I did, too," said Jim. "But that's another thing: You're always learning. Like tonight I was in the living room watching a football game, and we have this bathroom off to the side. Actually, a half bath because it doesn't have a tub, which some claim might cost you on the resale, but others believe new kitchen countertops—"

"Jim!" begged Serge. "We're grasping for knowledge! In God's name, focus!"

". . . But anyway, I leave the bathroom door open so I can still hear the play-by-play, and right in the middle of doing my business, I hear the announcer go nuts, the halfback is in the open, racing down the right side for the tying score. So naturally I look over my shoulder to see the touchdown. And wouldn't you know it? Martha picks that exact moment to walk by, and she yells, 'Jim!' And I say, 'What?' And she detonates, but I still don't know what I've done."

"What *did* you do?"

"What did he do?" said City. "He wasn't paying attention!"

"But it was a touchdown," said Serge.

"So football's more important than his wife?" said Country.

"But it was the tying score," said Coleman.

"It's just a stupid game," said City. "He needs to keep his eyes on the bowl at all times."

Serge scoffed. "It's not like he's capturing a rattlesnake."

"It's worse!" said City. "It's symbolic of his disrespect for her contributions to their union."

Jim sagged against the table. "That's what Martha said."

"What about the explaining?" asked Serge.

"She said if I really wanted to see the touchdown, I could have stopped going."

"But you can't stop the stream," said Serge.

"Yes he could have," said City.

"It's impossible," said Coleman.

"No it's not," said Country. "Men just don't want to make the commitment."

Serge shook his head and turned back to Jim. "You were saying?"

"So then I tried explaining that it was no big deal, meaning if there were any drops, I could quickly wipe them up, but she took it to mean that all her hard work keeping the house nice was no big deal."

"That's an easy one," said Serge. "With women, you don't get to pick the meaning of what you mean. They do. All men understand this."

"What's that supposed to mean?" said Country.

"It means that when you're arguing, you have to watch your words carefully."

"You just don't respect women," said City.

"That's not what I meant," said Serge.

"Don't try to take back what you said!"

Serge sighed. "I think we've made a breakthrough. Up to now, the division between the sexes was this: liking and not liking the Three Stooges. Who would have thought it was actually touchdowns and peeing?"

Country offered the whiskey bottle. "Another round, Jim?"

He shook his head. "Better not on an empty stomach."

Serge slapped his forehead. "Where's our hospitality? The first guest to our new family castle and we haven't offered him anything . . . Coleman, get him something to eat."

"Like what?"

"Anything." Serge stood. "Country, come with me. I want to show you something. I'm taking Christmas big!"

They left the table and walked around the corner.

A half hour passed.

"Serge? . . ." said Coleman. "Serge, where are you?" He walked through the kitchen. "Serge? . . ."

He turned down the hall and stopped. There they were beneath the mistletoe. Serge and Country, buck naked on the hardwood floor humping their brains out.

" . . . *Yes! . . . Faster! . . .*" Country's teeth gnashed. "*. . . Harder! Fuck it harder! . . .*"

"Serge," said Coleman, "I thought you were just supposed to kiss beneath the mistletoe."

Serge looked up and smiled. "I'm taking Christmas big! . . . Why are you interrupting us?"

"It's Jim," said Coleman. "I think we might have a problem."

CHAPTER NINE

MR. DAVENPORT

Serge jumped up. "What's the matter with Jim? What kind of problem?"

Coleman pointed back in the general direction of the living room. "You need to come see."

Serge zipped up some shorts. "Country, don't move. I'll be right back."

Coleman led the way. "He's in here."

The pair approached the living room. "What's that music?" said Serge. "It isn't the Christmas tunes I had on the stereo."

They turned the corner. Jim sat cross-legged on the floor.

"What's he doing?" asked Serge.

"Going through your Led Zeppelin CDs."

"*. . . Hey, hey, mama, said the way you move . . .*"

Jim looked up. "This is the most excellent music I've heard in my entire life."

"Jim?" Serge took a step forward. "Are you okay?"

"Listen to that time signature, man!" Jim slowly curved his arms apart in the air. "Drums go one way and the guitar blasts off in another, and then every few measures they meet up perfectly, like it was always meant to be—" Jim stopped and became racked with uncontrollable giggles.

"Coleman," said Serge. "His eyes are all bloodshot. What did you do to him?"

"Nothing. We were all just sitting around the table, and he suddenly started acting weird."

Serge looked over at the table. In front of Jim's chair was a serving plate full of gingerbread crumbs. "Coleman, please tell me you didn't give him the gingerbread house. It's got pot in the walls."

"You just said to feed him. It's all we had."

"Baby Jesus! What's Martha going to say when she finds him in this condition?"

"Maybe we can get him into bed before she finds out, and he can sleep it off."

"Good thinking." Serge bent down and grabbed Jim under one of his arms. "Help me get him up."

Coleman grabbed the other. "He's heavy."

"Jim," said Serge. "Time to be getting home, big boy."

Jim pointed back at the stereo as they guided him toward the door. "But 'Stairway to Heaven' . . ."

Serge helped him crawl under the Christmas tree. "I'm afraid right now they're playing 'Stairway to Your Bedroom.'"

The pair steadied Jim as they walked him across Triggerfish Lane. Jim's head lolled to the left. "I know you. You're Serge."

"Just keep on the way you're going, one foot in front of the other."

Jim looked ahead. "That's a big house. And I own it. There are a lot of electrical wires in the attic connecting everything. Far out."

"He's completely baked," said Coleman.

"Don't think we're not talking about this later."

They made it up the steps. "Get his keys."

"They're in this pocket," said Coleman.

Serge quietly opened the door and peeked inside.

"Why are you worried?" asked Coleman. "Martha's not home."

"But Nicole might be." Serge tugged Jim forward and tiptoed. "She can't see her dad like this. On the other hand, I did help her with the tattoo, so she might play ball."

"There are the stairs," said Coleman.

It was slow going, but they finally made it to the landing.

"What's that music?" asked Coleman.

"Coming from behind that closed door," said Serge. "Must be Nicole's room. We're in luck. Let's hurry and get him under the covers."

They hustled Jim into the master bedroom.

"Just lie down." Serge began taking off Jim's shoes.

Jim sat up. "But I don't want to. Music . . . I heard music . . ."

Serge pushed him back onto the mattress and pulled off his socks. "You've had a big day."

"Let's go," said Coleman.

"Husbands don't sleep in street clothes," said Serge. "Martha will know something's up. What do you think he wears to bed?"

"I don't know. His underwear?"

"Good enough."

They undressed Jim down to his skivvies and tucked him under the sheets. He snuggled the pillow and closed his eyes. Serge stood and took a deep breath. "Whew, that was fun-tastic. Let's get moving before Martha gets back."

They returned to their rental house. City and Country were dancing in the living room to Madonna.

"*. . . Respect yourself . . . Hey, hey! . . .*"

"Yo, Serge." Country passed City a joint. "What got into Jim?"

"Like you don't know. And turn down that music! Want all the neighbors to call the cops?"

Coleman stood at the front window. "They may call them anyway."

"Why?" said Serge. "What's going on?"

"See for yourself."

Serge looked outside at Jim standing in the middle of the street in his underwear. "Shit, we got to get him back inside!"

They ran toward the road. "Jim, what the hell are you doing?"

Jim swayed and stared straight up. "Look at all the stars. We're so insignificant."

"Coleman, grab his other arm."

Coleman glanced down. "Serge, I think he has a hard-on."

"Just let's get him back in bed."

Minutes later, Jim was under the covers again with eyes closed. "Time to split," said Serge. "And hope the Happy Wanderer stays put."

They ran back across the street.

Coleman got on his hands and knees in front of the Christmas tree. "Serge, aren't you coming?"

"Just a minute." He stood and faced the house across the street. "I want to make sure he remains down this time."

They watched and waited.

"Dammit," said Serge. "A light just came on."

"Where?"

"I think it's the kitchen."

"Maybe it's Nicole."

"We should be that lucky." Serge took off.

No stealth this round, galloping through the front door. Serge's feet hit the brakes in the kitchen doorway. "Jim, dear God, look at you!"

Coleman tapped his shoulder. "Serge . . ."

"Not now." Serge swatted his hand away. "Jim, I know it's not your fault, but you've got to pull it together."

A tap on his shoulder. "Serge . . ."

"Stop it, Coleman . . . Jim, look alive! Martha's going to be home any minute."

Another tap. "Serge . . ."

"What!"

"She *is* home."

Serge's eyes darted toward the front door. Keys jingling. "Coleman, quick. We need to find the back way out."

"Where is it?"

"I don't know."

The knob began turning.

"No time," said Serge. "This way! . . ."

They dashed out of sight just as the front door opened. Martha flicked on the lights. "Jim? . . . Jim, I'm sorry we had a fight . . ." Walking through the living room. "Jim? Are you still up?" She reached the kitchen doorway . . .

"What in the name of . . . Jim? . . . I . . . you . . . Jim? . . ."

Jim looked up with a silly smile. Sitting on the kitchen floor in his underwear. In front of an open refrigerator. Eating leftovers with his bare hands.

"Martha, did I ever tell you you're the best cook in the entire world?"

Nicole came running down the stairs. "Mom, I heard you yell. Is everything okay?"

"No! Look at your father!"

Nicole's mouth fell open. She looked at the drumsticks in each hand, then his eyes. She covered her mouth. "Oh my God! Daddy's . . ."

"Daddy's what?" demanded Martha.

"Uh, Daddy's hungry. Yeah, that's it."

"I've never seen him like this." Martha grabbed the drumsticks and put them back in their Rubbermaid container. "Something's not right."

"He started having a pretty bad cough," Nicole said quickly, thinking on her feet. "I think he took some of that syrup in the medicine cabinet."

"You mean the prescription? But he hates to take that stuff. Says it makes him loopy."

Nicole shrugged. "It was a pretty bad cough."

Martha looked down. "Is that what happened?"

Jim looked up. A loopy grin.

"Okay, let's get you to bed."

Martha got Jim to his feet and walked him up the stairs. Nicole followed, having the time of her young life.

A half hour deeper into the night.

The master bedroom of the Davenport residence. A woman's voice:

"*. . . Oh Jim! . . . Oh God! . . . Don't stop! . . . Yes! Yes! . . .*"

The sheets moved up and down in the moonlight pouring from the south window.

"*. . . Jim! . . . Where'd you learn that? . . . You've never been this good! . . . Oh yes! . . . Do it again! . . . Yes! Yes! Yes! . . .*"

"Serge," whispered Coleman. "They're really going at it."

"Stop listening to them," said Serge. "It's rude."

"Must be the pot he took."

"And stop whispering. She might hear you."

"*. . . Oh yes! . . . Oh God! . . .*"

"Serge?"

"What!"

"Why did we run up the stairs instead of taking off out the back?"

"Because Martha was just about to come through the front door, and there wasn't enough time to make it down the hall without her seeing us." Serge checked his glowing wristwatch in the dark. "Was hoping we could open a window and climb onto the roof, but they were all stuck."

"And we ended up in the bathroom shower with the curtain pulled?"

"Too much clothes in the closet."

"So what do we do?"

"Sit tight in this bathtub until they fall asleep. Then creep out like thieves."

"I think they stopped." Coleman strained to listen. "Yes, they've definitely stopped."

"No more talking." Serge eased himself down onto the bathtub and checked his watch again.

The night wore on.

Serge's closed eyes fluttered open. He shook the fog from his head. "Must have dozed off. What time is it?" He checked his watch. "Four-thirty? Time to be going." He started getting up. "Coleman? You awake? . . . Coleman?" He reached out in the darkness and felt only air. "Coleman, where are you?"

Then a familiar sound.

Serge grabbed the hair on his own head and pulled. "Fuck me." He yanked the shower curtain back and stuck his head out. "Coleman, what the hell do you think you're doing?"

"I have to pee."

"Stop!" he whispered harshly. "She might hear you!"

"I can't. The stream's already started."

"So cut it off!"

"It's impossible—"

The door suddenly opened and the lights came on.

Martha stood in shock at what she saw: Serge's head poking out from the shower curtains, and Coleman standing at the toilet, looking back over his shoulder at her, his piss stream spraying all over the floor.

Serge grinned sheepishly. "I can explain."

CHAPTER TEN

THE NEXT DAY

Serge stared out the front window with binoculars. "Man, I've never seen a woman as mad as Martha. And I've seen a lot of women mad."

"She yelled at us way too much."

"Coleman, after all we talked about over here, did you have to pee on her floor?"

"I think she was mainly mad that we were just there."

"But what made you tell her you tried hard not to hear them banging each other?"

"I thought that would be a nice thing to say."

"For future reference, any random sentence from a library is nicer."

"I'm just glad she didn't call the cops," said Coleman.

"She would have," said Serge. "Thank heavens Jim and Nicole were there to talk her down from that idea."

From behind: "You guys are buffoons."

"Great," said Serge. "Taking it from all angles." He lowered his binoculars. "I need to find a way to make it up to them . . . Coleman, stop staring over there. How many times do I have to tell you?"

"But City and Country are making out. I can't help it."

City looked over at Coleman. "Why don't you take a picture? It'll last longer."

"Serge, can I borrow your camera?"

"Shut up!"

"I didn't know they were lesbians."

Serge raised his binoculars again. "They're not."

"But they're making out."

"That's because City's current other option is you."

"You mean they're doing that for me?"

"Uh, yeah, Coleman. That's exactly what's going on."

"Do you think they'll take requests?"

"Coleman, just . . . hold on, what's this?"

"What do you see?"

"It's that Ram pickup again." Serge shortened up the focus on his binoculars. "One of the vehicles from yesterday. It's the third time I've seen it on the street today."

"What's it doing?"

"Slowing down and looking at Jim's house. It's like he's casing the place." Serge pulled a cell phone from his pocket. "I don't like the looks of this."

"Who are you calling?"

"Shhhhhh! It's ringing . . . Jim? Me, Serge. Don't hang up! . . . Something important might be happening . . . Well, like, do you have any enemies? . . . Given your demeanor, I didn't think so . . . How about your job? What kind of consulting do you actually do? . . . What do you mean you don't do any consulting? Then what do they pay you for . . . Could you repeat that last part again? . . . Why didn't you tell me that before? . . . Just relax and forget I called." He hung up. "Damn."

"What is it?" asked Coleman.

Serge walked across the room. "Jim's life is in danger. I just found out he's a consultant."

"Someone mad he gave bad advice?"

"Worse. He's with one of those companies that fires people by proxy to take the heat." Serge arrived at a box of clothes. "That pickup made its last pass at sunset. He's waiting for dark. So the next step is obvious."

"You don't mean—"

"That's right." Serge reached in the box and pulled out a green felt hat.

Just after nightfall.

Two green hats poked out from behind a palm tree on Triggerfish Lane.

Looking across the street at the Davenport residence.

"I don't see anything yet," said Coleman. "Are you sure about this hunch?"

"Never been more sure about anything in my life, except all the times I was more sure and was wrong, so they don't count."

"Then I think you should warn Jim. Just in case."

"I'm not exactly excited about going anywhere near that house after last night."

"But Martha's car is gone. It's your chance."

"You may be right." Serge stepped out from behind the palm tree. "This is too important . . . But stay alert. If you see Martha coming back, give me a secret signal."

"Like what?"

"I don't know. Yell something in code that only I will be able to interpret."

Serge ran across their yard, then the street, then Jim's yard, and up the porch steps.

Ding-dong, ding-dong, ding-dong—

Jim opened the door.

Yet another gasp.

"Don't close the door!" said Serge. "I know how you must feel about us listening to you fuck and peeing on your floor, especially so close to Christmas, but I have something important to tell you . . ."

"Dang it, Serge! Martha's going to be home any minute!"

"And it will only take a minute."

Jim stuck his head outside and looked up the street. "She can't see you out here." He jerked Serge inside and closed the door. "Now what's going on?"

"I think someone you may have fired—"

Headlights swept through the living room window.

"That's her coming up the driveway now!" said Jim.

Coleman's faint voice from across the street. *"Serge! Martha's coming!"*

Jim grabbed Serge by the shoulders. "You have to get out of here. And no upstairs this time. The back door's right down that hall."

"You got it." Serge took off and disappeared out the rear just as Martha came in the front.

. . . Back across the street, a green hat poked from behind a palm tree. Coleman watched as Serge crept along the side of the Davenports' house, peeking around the front to make sure the coast was clear, then dashing back across Triggerfish Lane.

He rejoined his buddy behind the palm tree, grabbing his knees and panting.

"Did Martha see you?"

Serge shook his head. "But it was too close for comfort."

Coleman sniffed the air. "What's that smell?"

Serge sniffed with him. "What *is* that smell?" He checked the bottoms of his elf shoes. "Dammit."

"What's the matter?" asked Coleman.

"I think I just tracked dog shit all through their house."

"You forgot to wipe your feet?"

"And so close to Christmas—"

Suddenly yelling erupted across the road. The front door opened. Jim stepped outside and turned around to say something. The door slammed shut. Jim checked the bottoms of his shoes.

"Pssssst!" Serge stood beside the palm tree, urgently waving Jim over.

Jim slowly crossed Triggerfish Lane and stopped a few feet in front of Serge. He just stared.

"Is Martha mad?" asked Serge.

Continued staring.

"Maybe it's been a long time since you took her out to dinner."

"Serge! There's dog crap all over the house!"

"And that just isn't correct," said Serge. "Someone around here is walking their pets and not cleaning up behind. I'll keep an eye out for who's responsible—"

"Serge!"

"Jim, I think your life might be in danger. I've seen several vehicles casing your house, especially this one Ram pickup."

"I know you're just trying to help, but please stop helping!" Jim walked toward his house.

Serge grabbed him from behind.

Jim turned around. "I told you I don't want your help."

"No, look." Serge pointed up the street. "That pickup truck's coming back. Quick! Behind the palm tree!"

They all watched as the Dodge Ram slowly rolled to a stop at the curb in front of Serge's rental house.

"Is that a blue parking sticker on the windshield?" asked Jim.

"The streetlights sometimes play tricks," said Serge. "But looks blue to me."

"I think it's from a distribution warehouse in Lakeland where I fired some people a few days ago."

"Shhhh!" said Serge. "He just turned the cab light on."

Inside the pickup, a man in a trucker cap guzzled straight from a nearly empty bottle of Smirnoff. Then held a .44 Magnum revolver in front of his face, popped out the cylinder, and inserted bullets.

"Vodka and guns," said Serge. "I hate to be the suspicious type, but that's not a rabbit's foot."

The pickup's door opened and the driver got out. They heard indistinct muttering. Cowboy boots staggered across the street, gun swinging by his side.

Jim jumped from behind the palm tree. "Martha's still home!"

Serge grabbed him again. "Jim, you don't have the training. You'll just get yourself shot."

"But my wife—"

"I'm on it," said Serge. "I've done this a million times, so nothing possibly can go wrong . . ."

Cowboy boots stomped up the porch steps. They staggered back, then forward again. An unsteady index finger circled the doorbell button until it finally found its mark.

Ding-dong.

Just then, the man in the trucker's cap heard quickly approaching jingle bells. He spun around and looked down at elf shoes. "What the hell—"

Serge swiftly grabbed a giant terra-cotta flowerpot off the porch and smashed the man on the side of the head. Then he socked him in the jaw. The man went backward, losing his balance. He crashed through the side porch railing and landed unconscious between a tall hedge and the house.

Serge sniffed the air. He lifted his left leg by the ankle and checked the bottom of his shoe. "Damn."

The door opened. Martha stood speechless, looking at a porch covered with broken pottery, busted pieces of porch railing, and Serge in an elf suit with a green shoe caked in poop.

He lowered his leg. "I can explain."

Five minutes later.

Three heads poked out from behind a palm tree. Martha screeched backward out of the driveway and sped off down Triggerfish Lane.

"Excellent," said Serge.

"You call this excellent?" said Jim. "Martha's a hair from divorcing me if she doesn't crash the car first, my porch is half destroyed, and there's a drunk guy with a huge gun somewhere in the shrubs."

"All in a day," said Serge. "With Martha gone, it's an excellent time to get the guy out of there. Imagine if she stayed home and saw us dragging him unconscious across the lawn with a .44 Magnum. Hallmark doesn't make that kind of card."

Jim grabbed his head with both hands and rocked feverishly. "Ooooo, it's starting again. It's just like the last time . . ."

Serge pulled Jim's arms down. "You have to get a grip."

"But every time you enter my life . . ."

"And every time I save you, right?" Serge lifted Jim's chin. "Am I right or not?"

"No, you're right. It's just the stress."

"Here's the plan," said Serge. "Go back home and act like nothing happened."

"What are you going to do?"

"You don't want to know," said Serge. "In fact, forget there ever was a guy."

"How am I supposed to forget something like that?"

"I don't know," said Serge. "Get busy doing something to take your mind off it. I'm sure your floors could use a good going over."

CHAPTER ELEVEN

MIDNIGHT

A '72 Chevelle raced east on Interstate 4.

Past the exit for the annual strawberry festival in Plant City. A dinosaur statue advertised a roadside attraction of more dinosaur statues. An RV dealership tried to lure customers from the highway with a row of silver Airstream trailers buried halfway in the ground straight up.

Serge took an off-ramp for Lakeland. He held a driver's license under the map light and navigated through the streets for an address.

"Good, it's rural." Serge cruised slowly through a sparse neighborhood with drainage ditches near the road and no sidewalk. He slowed and double-checked the street number again. "This is the place."

The Chevelle backed into the driveway. The trunk opened. Serge grabbed wrists.

Coleman grabbed ankles. "How many times have we done this?"

"I've lost count."

"He's heavier than most."

Twenty minutes later. Thick ropes tied cowboy boots to the legs of a wooden chair, sitting alone in the middle of a dark living room. More ropes around his chest and hands.

Serge was faced the other way, on his knees, assembling another unique . . . well, what the hell was it?

"Serge." Coleman tossed back some pills. "What the hell is it?"

"You'll see." More twisting, pressing, clamping. Reaching for additional parts.

"Where'd you get all that stuff?"

"Toy Town. It was supposed to be a few of my Secret Santa presents for you, but something came up."

"Don't those toys go separately?"

"That's what most people think." Further assembly. "The power structure starts boxing in your mind when you're small. People think these are just toys, but they're also agents of mind control. Luckily I broke the chains early." Serge snapped a final piece in place and stood proudly. "Judge for yourself. The fruits of a free individual."

"I don't get it. Looks like those modern art things at the museums you always drag me to. I don't get those either."

"The free-thinkers will get it."

Muted screaming from across the room. Serge turned and faced the hostage. "Maybe he's a free-thinker. Let's find out!"

Serge skipped across the room and pulled the duct tape off his mouth.

"Ow!"

Serge gestured at his creation. "Tell me what you think. Your honest opinion, don't hold back. And don't be embarrassed if you don't get it. They probably got to you early with the toys."

"I swear, I wasn't going to do anything to Jim." Tears streaming down cheeks. "I only wanted some answers."

"Then what was the gun for?"

"That was just to scare him. Please don't hurt me!"

"Why would you say something like that?"

"Because . . . that *thing*."

Serge glanced across the room. "Looks harmless enough to me."

"Listen, if you let me go, I swear you'll never see me again." Chest heaving. "I'll forget Jim ever existed."

"Really?" Serge nodded to himself. "That sounds awfully generous of you."

"Oh, thank you. You won't be sorry."

"And you probably even believe that yourself." Serge tore off a new stretch of duct tape and strapped it around his mouth. "The problem is that you're an unknown variable."

"Serge?" Coleman took a big sucking hit on a joint. "What's an unknown . . . that other word you used?"

"Some people you can reason with. Others you have to threaten, but even most of those respond logically to the threats. They behave in a predictable pattern." Serge walked back across the room and joined Coleman. "But this loser doesn't know what he's going to do next, so how can we? As long as he's out there, a decent family isn't safe."

"And now I get to see what your device does?"

"Not yet." Serge looked down at his curled green toes. "I paid a lot for these elf suits. I'd like to get some use out of them."

"What do you have in mind?"

"Since we have an audience, how about a song-and-dance routine?"

Coleman took another big hit and set it down in an ashtray. "Lead on."

"And I'll need that joint."

"But you don't get high," said Coleman.

"There are other uses." And Serge put it to use.

"Oh, yeah," said Coleman. "Cool."

"Ready?"

Serge and Coleman stood side by side in front of the hostage, wiggling against the ropes and squealing under the tape.

"What do I do?" asked Coleman.

"Just put your hands on your hips and kick those bell-fringed shoes out in a merry jig. We'll make up the song as we go along."

The pair began kicking and jingling.

Serge: *"A one, and a two and . . . Ohhhhhh, what the heck can that contraption be?"*

Coleman: *"What the fuck's going to happen to me?"*

Serge: *"These crazy elves are all over the map."*

Coleman: *"But don't have a cow, and don't you crap."*

Serge: *"Because Santa Claus is cominnnnnnng . . . to town!"*

TWO HOURS LATER

The 911 calls came in all at once. At least a dozen neighbors.

And even more sheriff's cruisers, parked helter-skelter across the front yard of a rural home in Lakeland.

People stood on front lawns in nightgowns and pajamas. A news truck arrived.

Detectives climbed out of a white Crown Vic and approached the crime tape.

A deputy stood beside the door. "Hope you haven't eaten anything big lately."

"What have we got in there?" asked the lead detective.

"Medical examiner's already inside."

The detectives ducked under the yellow ribbon.

"Jesus! . . ."

A large knot of forensic people worked in a careful choreography to keep out of one another's way as they worked around the body. Camera flashes, tweezers, evidence bags.

The detectives turned in the other direction. A long scorch mark up the wall and a larger one across the floor toward the victim's chair.

The medical examiner came over. "Caught a break. The explosion woke up the whole street, so we got the scene fresh."

"What are all those things sticking out of him?" asked the head detective. "And the wall behind?"

"Shrapnel. Still taking inventory. And we're sure to find more inside when we do the autopsy, but so far . . ." He referred to his clipboard. "We count twenty-seven LEGO blocks; nineteen Tinkertoys, both the sticks and the wheel things; thirty-one Erector Set beams; and a Lincoln Log through his left lung."

"Holy mother," said the detective. "He must have used plastique or ammonium nitrate."

The examiner shook his head. "Just standard black powder." He held up an evidence bag containing the nub of a joint. "This was the fuse."

"Wait a second," said the detective. "I've seen black powder before, and there's no way it could generate this force . . ." He stopped and realized something new. "How come the debris is only concentrated in that one area toward the chair?"

"The same reason it was so powerful." The medical examiner sketched on his clipboard. "I used to be in the army. This is what we'd call a shaped, directional charge. It's the difference between a bomb and a cannon. A small amount of black powder goes a lot further when the release is concentrated in a tight vector."

"But how did they do it?"

He sketched some more. "The key was the LEGOs. He interlocked multiple walls on the desired sides for maximum delivery. Our guy clearly had demolition training."

"Just great," said the detective. "Any witnesses?"

"One of the neighbors across the street said he saw two guys getting into a car shortly before hearing the blast."

"Were they from around here?"

"The neighbor seriously doubts it because of the way they were dressed," said the examiner. "When he first told us, we gave him the Breathalyzer, but he passed."

"So how were they dressed?"

"You're not going to believe this."

CHAPTER TWELVE

TAMPA BAY MALL

The weekend before Christmas. Parking lot packed. Baby strollers, parents with boxes and shopping bags. Some cars followed people leaving the stores, hoping to grab their space.

A '72 Chevelle rolled down a long line of vehicles. It was not looking for a space.

"If we're not looking for a space, then what are we doing here?" asked Coleman.

"Working." Serge leaned over the wheel, carefully making a U-turn at the end of the row and heading back up another.

"But we usually only steal from other crooks or rich assholes." Coleman took a slug from a pint flask. "We don't mess with regular folk."

"And we're not about to start."

"But you said work—"

"Hold it," said Serge. "Up ahead at eleven o'clock. That pair of police cars. Our cue to leave."

"Good thinking," said Coleman. "Don't want them to catch us."

"That's not why we're leaving." Serge left the parking lot and headed for I-275. "Those police cars mean they're doing our work for us."

"I don't follow."

"Starting the day after Thanksgiving, at malls all across Florida, thieves descend in droves on the parking lots. The reasons are many: more targets, more expensive gift items, shoppers distracted by the holiday hubbub, and added chaos in which to escape. Next time you're hitting the shopping centers around Christmas, count all the police cars, and the bad guys."

"How do you spot the bad guys?"

"The smart ones are on foot, camouflaged among the shoppers, and can usually only be spotted when they're entering the lot from the street. The dumb ones ride bicycles. I mean, who rides bicycles up and down rows of cars at the mall? And it only happens around Christmas. It's like they get some kind of newsletter."

They headed northeast to one of the older malls in the suburbs. "But the scariest ones are in cars," said Serge. "Some of them also take the customer. One woman was snatched in broad daylight on a Saturday, and they found her body in an orange grove outside Wauchula. That's the thing about Christmas: all the memories."

"I remember getting G.I. Joes when they were at their peak," said Coleman.

"Me, too!" said Serge. "I spotted them under the tree at two A.M. and woke my parents. They told me it was too early and to go back to sleep, but I stomped my feet and flapped my arms: 'There are G.I. Joes out there!' That was the pattern: I'd always wake up early and sneak out to see if Santa had come yet. But you had to be careful, because if he was there and still working, you just never knew. There were stories floating around about coal in stockings. Little kids wait a whole year for Christmas, which is like ten adult years, and then coal. So you knew he could also be an asshole."

"And you knew he really existed because he ate the cookies and drank the milk."

"Once when I was little, I did something bad. My mom made a fake phone call to Santa, and I lost my fucking mind." Serge turned into the parking lot of another mall. "She thought it would just worry me a little and I'd behave, but Santa is the religion of children. You don't go there. She's telling Santa not to bring me any presents, and I flipped out as if you threw a cat in a shower, screaming and jumping all over the place, and I finally scooted a chair over. The phone was one of those old wall units. Or at least until I ripped it down, and my mom went speechless, just staring at me lying on the floor with the wall unit clutched to my chest, going, 'Don't you ever call Santa on me!' I was only four, but she didn't call again."

Coleman rolled down his window to flick a joint ash.

"Coleman!" said Serge. "Be more careful! Your elf hat could blow off."

"It's on tight," said Coleman. "Ever stick your tongue on a flagpole?"

"Why would I do that?"

"Because it's supposed to freeze." Coleman unscrewed his flask. "I even tried it once, but we were living in Florida. It just tasted bad."

"I came down with the mumps one Christmas." Serge veered around the movie-plex. "And you never hear about them anymore. You hear about measles and chicken pox, but it's hush-hush about mumps."

"Some shit's going down somewhere."

"That's my guess. Another memory was being the first kid in the neighborhood who figured out there wasn't a Santa, and the other kids tried to suppress my message. I didn't fit in for a couple years, like if you're an atheist today, or in the ACLU. Remember Advent calendars?"

"Can't place it."

"That means you weren't Catholic," said Serge. "We'd get these cool cardboard calendars that marked off the days to Christmas, and each day you'd open a little perforated window and get a piece of chocolate. There was a lot of bribery in the Catholic Church."

"I'm not seeing any police cars," said Coleman.

"Me neither," said Serge. "But lots of people on bicycles. Looks like we have a gig."

"The people on bikes are riding between cars."

"To look in backseats for presents people bought elsewhere before coming here." Serge leaned on the horn.

"Look at the bicycles scatter," said Coleman.

"They'll just regroup a few rows over like pigeons."

"Over there," said Coleman. "I think I see a real elf."

"Where?"

"Next row. We just passed him."

Serge reached the edge of the parking lot and doubled back. "I see him. He's fiddling with something in the trunk of his car. Except I don't think that's a real elf."

"But he's got the bright green elf suit and jingle-bell shoes and everything," said Coleman. "Why else would he be dressed like that?"

"To do what we're doing," said Serge. "Blend in."

"He's looking awfully suspicious. Head jerking around, constantly looking behind him."

"He's just pretending to fiddle in his trunk." Serge applied the brake and pulled out binoculars. "He's really waiting for prey to walk by . . . Which brings up an ethical dilemma for me."

"What's that?"

Serge patted the chest of his own green costume. "Should I give him a pass out of professional courtesy?"

"I'd say it depends on what he does."

"Reasonable call." Serge tightened the view on his binoculars. "And here comes a young woman now, loaded down with packages."

"He's glancing at her."

"I don't like this," said Serge. "He's a big strong guy, and if he wasn't dressed that way, she'd be on the Women's Parking Lot Alert Status. But now her guard's down. He's taking advantage of her favorable view of elves."

Serge took his foot off the brake and idled forward.

"She's closer," said Coleman. "Looks like he's getting ready. You'll need to speed up."

"No," said Serge. "I have to make sure we're right about his intentions. If I'm wrong and we strike too soon, we could needlessly freak her out by having her witness an elf fight. It's an ugly thing to see."

"Serge, he's making his move! He's going for the packages!"

"He's not going for the packages. He's just knocking them out of her arms." Serge hit the gas. "He's going for her! He's got her around the waist. It's an abduction!"

"She's kicking her legs like crazy," said Coleman. "He's throwing her in the trunk. He slammed the hood shut!"

The kidnapping elf ran for his driver's door and jumped in. Before he could back out, a Chevelle screeched up and boxed him in. Serge and Coleman leaped out and ran to the driver's side. A punch through the open window.

Coleman opened the door, and Serge dragged the would-be abductor out of the car by his hair and threw him to the ground. The assailant crawled toward the back of the car as Serge kicked him in the ribs. The man finally got to his feet and took a swing at Coleman, missing wildly. Serge grabbed him and threw him over the hood of the Chevelle. The man jumped back up and pulled a knife, but Serge kicked it out of his hand. Then he delivered a nasty head butt, dropping the man to the pavement. Serge began stomping the daylights out of him.

In the distance, people coming out of the mall began to point.

"Elf fight! Elf fight!"

"Looks like the fat one's peeing on him."

"It's an ugly thing to see."

Back at the Chevelle, Serge had the trunk open. They threw the man in and slammed the hood.

Then they ran over to the kidnapper's car. Serge had the man's keys and popped the trunk.

A terrified woman shielded her eyes against the bright Florida sun, looking up at two men in green felt hats. "Don't hurt me!"

"We're not going to hurt you. We're rescuing you." Serge extended a hand to help her out of the car. "Please don't judge all elves by this one incident."

They hopped back in the Chevelle and sped off.

CHAPTER THIRTEEN

THE NEXT MORNING

Extra early.

"Come on, Coleman! I got the engine running!"

Coleman stumbled out the door, pulling up his elf pants. "Why so early?"

"Because it's the Christmas shopping season. Everyone knows all the best sales are early."

Coleman climbed in. "You mean the ones I see on TV where a million people wait outside the store for the doors to open?"

"That's right, mainly loving parents who sacrifice their sleep to make sure their child gets the year's most popular new toy." Serge threw the Chevelle in gear. "Then the store opens and they rip each other to pieces."

The pair cruised up Dale Mabry Highway in the predawn twilight. Heavy traffic. Other shoppers and people with early-shift jobs—Dunkin' Donuts, tollbooths, filling newspaper racks. Coleman smoked fake incense sold in head shops.

"I love this time of day," said Serge. "The majesty of approaching dawn."

"I know exactly what you mean." Coleman puffed a fat one in the passenger seat. "Because if you like to get stoned, it involves a sleep commitment, and you usually only see the sun go down. But if for some reason you're up now and get stoned before the sun rises, it blows out your tubes, like this one guy I knew was on acid and saw the sun go down in the evening, but LSD keeps you up all night, and then we went to the beach to see the sun rise, and he yells, 'Look! The freakin' sunset is going in reverse! We're traveling back in time! I'm getting younger! I'm going back in the womb!' Then he jumped in the ocean, and we found him an hour later hiding under the pier with all these jellyfish stings, crying and trying to bury himself in the sand. Man, that guy was seriously fucked up . . . What? You're staring at me."

Serge looked at Coleman another moment, then back at the road. "I was just trying to say sunrises are pretty."

"So where is this big sale, anyway?"

"Mega Deals."

"You mean that giant place that sells electronics and video games super cheap?"

"That's right," said Serge. "They're selling the first one hundred Play-Box Fours for ninety-nine dollars. Whatever happened to real toys? Or just running around the woods with sticks. But today, kids asks Santa for a fortune in swag. What did you used to ask Santa for?"

Coleman exhaled a hit out the window. "Nothing."

"How could you ask for nothing?"

"Because I was whining and kicking the whole time. The whole business of tossing a kid in some weirdo's lap creeped me out."

"One year I only asked for two things, because they were the things I really needed," said Serge. "Keep it simple so there wouldn't be any screwup."

"Needed?"

"Frosty the Snowcone Machine and the Matchbox car suitcase."

"What for?"

"Survival. It was 1965, and we'd just ridden out Hurricane Betsy." Serge joined a long line of traffic with blinkers turning into an enormous parking lot. "Guess it scarred me. It was a different time back then: People didn't evacuate like they do now, just like they also didn't wear seat belts and sold candy cigarettes to children. I was afraid my family and the neighbors might be wiped out by another storm or nuclear attack—they were still talking about that on TV at the time because the Cuban Missile Crisis was only three years earlier—and I'd have to survive on my own. I really sweated out those last months till Christmas. And that Christmas morning was more relief than joy. I'm like, 'Whew! Now I can survive.' I got the snowcone machine. You can get ice anywhere, and the machine came with flavor packets, so I'll be able to eat, and I ripped the dividers out of the Matchbox case and filled it with clothes and a toothbrush, and hid it under my bed for emergency departure. And before dark every night, I made sure my tricycle was pointed out of the driveway. Then I'd conduct drills each week, racing from the house and throwing the little suitcase and Frosty in the tricycle's basket and take off up the sidewalk. My folks later told me they'd stand in the window, thinking, 'Look at that intense expression on his face. And look at him pedal! It's almost like his life depends on it.'"

"You always have a plan."

"But the one thing I don't have is the Christmas memory I want most. I've never seen snow, not on December twenty-fifth or any other day. People find that outlandish, but among us who have lived our entire lives in Florida, it's actually quite common. And I even had my chance once. On January twentieth, 1977, there was like a super-rare two-hundred-year storm event, and it happened in my lifetime. It snowed all the way down to Miami Beach. Just tiny flurries and no accumulation, but it was snow, and the *Miami Herald* ran headlines like when man landed on the moon. Except I was inside or something and I missed it! . . . I'd give anything to see snow."

"Look!" said Coleman. "There must be a thousand people outside that store!"

"Speaking of which . . ." Serge pulled into a parking slot that seemed like a mile away. "You ready for this one? We're taking Christmas big!"

Coleman pushed his elf hat on tight. "Let's rock."

They got out, walked to the back of the Chevelle, and

popped the trunk. A third elf, bound and gagged, squirmed like a caterpillar. Serge grabbed the edge of the duct tape across the man's mouth. "Sleep well last night?" Then ripped the tape off, prompting a verbal deluge.

"Oh, please don't hurt me! I wasn't going to do anything to that woman! I swear! I'll do anything you want! Please don't hurt me!"

"Of course we won't hurt you," said Serge, producing a hypodermic needle from a shaving kit.

"W-w-what's that for?" asked the captive.

"Fun, fun, fun! . . . Coleman, where would a junkie inject? I wouldn't want to leave the false impression of foul play."

Coleman tapped the inside of the man's left arm. "That vein there."

Serge held the syringe upright, delicately pressing the plunger with his thumb until a bead of liquid dripped off the tip of the needle, then he stuck it where Coleman showed him and emptied half the chamber.

The hostage raised his head. "What was in that . . . ?" The sentence trailed off into merry humming.

"What *was* in that?" asked Coleman.

"Liquid Valium. I smashed up some of your pills."

"Serge!"

"Consider it your contribution to the War on Christmas." Serge grabbed an arm. "Now let's get him out of the trunk."

They got their captive upright and began guiding him slowly across the parking lot.

"Serge," said Coleman. "He's got spaghetti legs."

"Just don't let go."

The man continued humming and looked at Coleman with a hapless smile. "You have a funny hat."

They eventually finished traversing the parking lot.

"The crowd's even bigger than I thought!" said Coleman. "And we're way in the back. We'll never get in."

"Yes, we will."

"I don't see how? They're packed like sardines."

"You underestimate the power of the Christmas spirit. Just don't let go of him . . ." Serge raised his chin and his voice. "Elves coming through! Elves coming through! . . ."

The crowd magically parted, then closed back up behind them after they had passed.

"Serge, it's working."

"Elves here! Elves at work! . . ."

The trio reached the front of the crowd, which sandwiched them against the store's locked doors. Coleman's nose and cheek flattened against the glass. "These people are really pushing!"

"They must seriously want those Play-Boxes." Serge needed to check his wristwatch, and struggled to get his arm up to his face like he was in a straitjacket. "I have a minute to nine. And here comes the manager with the key. Just remember what I told you."

"My face is getting numb."

Just as the manager reached the door and began inserting his key:

"Excuse me!" Serge shouted back at the crowd. "I'm the

head elf at this store, and it is with deep regret that I must inform you we don't quite have one hundred Play-Boxes . . ." Serge paced his words as he watched the manager's key in slow motion. The lock clicked free. "We only have ten!"

Doors flew open and the mob charged.

The three elves were carried inside like surfers riding a wave, and it didn't stop until Serge and Coleman fell off the left side of the wave near car audio.

Coleman got up and brushed dust from his felt stomach. "That was a rush . . . Sorry about losing my hat."

"We lost something else," said Serge, standing on tiptoes and craning his neck.

"Where'd he go?" asked Coleman.

"Probably wants a Play-Box. Let's check out the DVDs."

THE NEXT DAY

Bayshore Manors.

A low-rise residential complex tucked between the towering condos along Tampa's Bayshore Boulevard.

It advertised an "active retirement lifestyle," but it was more of a rest home.

Occupants sat around the dayroom. The sole TV was playing *The View.*

A ninety-two-year-old woman shuffled across the terrazzo floor in slippers. She glanced around, concealing something inside her nightgown.

Three women about the same age waited on a sofa.

"Did you get it?" asked Edith.

Eunice looked back over her shoulder and nodded, then pulled a bottle from her nightgown. "Absolut. I bribed one of the therapists."

"I got the eggnog mix," said Ethel.

"Pour that shit," said Edna. "And don't be stingy."

Everyone got their serving, and Eunice stuffed the bottle between sofa cushions. They settled in.

Edith grabbed a morning paper. "Listen to this: 'Elf Trampled to Death in Holiday Sale Stampede.'"

"Every year the same headlines," said Eunice.

Edna frowned at the television. "What's happened to Barbara Walters?"

"I hate this show," said Ethel.

"I hate this whole place," said Edith.

"It's not so bad." Edna finished her glass. "Break out that bottle again."

"It's a terrible place," Edith emphasized. "The kind of joint where they stick you when they won't let you drive anymore."

"You *shouldn't* drive," said Ethel. "Last time you went the wrong way on the interstate. The semi missed us by inches."

"The traffic signs were confusing."

"'Do Not Enter,'" said Eunice. "Yeah, that's a mystery for the ages."

"I'm warning you!"

"Or what? You'll spit up on me?"

"That's it!" A cane came out.

"Girls! Girls!" said Edna, getting between them. "We

shouldn't be fighting with each other. We should be fight-ing them."

"Who?" asked Eunice.

Edna nodded across the room, toward a small group of young women chatting next to their supervisor's desk. "Our caregivers. Look at 'em so smug."

"Always condescending," said Ethel.

"And they always find our vodka," said Edith.

"But what are you going to do?" Eunice poured another cup. "We're practically prisoners here."

"No we're not," said Edith.

"But they won't let us drive anymore," said Edna.

"So what? You're not seeing the big picture. We're now free to do whatever we feel. Instead, we've sat around bitch-ing and moaning for the last six months."

"What's your point?"

"We're not responsible for ourselves anymore. The possi-bilities are endless," explained Edith. "We can do absolutely anything we want, and they'll just chalk it up to our age and ailments."

"Example?"

"Watch this: . . . Yoo-hoo!" She waved toward the care-givers' station as if she needed something.

Two spritely young women walked across the room. The one on the left bent down and smiled like a kindergarten teacher. "And how may I help you today?"

Edith smiled back. "Go fuck yourself."

The caregiver stood up and turned to her colleague. "Tourette's." They walked away.

Four women on the sofa snickered.

"Who's in?" said Edith.

"For what?" asked Eunice.

"An adventure," said Edith. "The world out there is our oyster."

"But we can't drive," said Edna.

"They took away our licenses, not our hands and feet."

"But we'll get in trouble."

"They'll just bring us back."

"So what's your plan?" asked Ethel.

"I know where they keep the keys to the shuttle bus."

"Let's do it," said Eunice.

"Grab the vodka," said Edith. "We're blowing this Popsicle stand."

CHAPTER FOURTEEN

TRIGGERFISH LANE

Two men in green outfits stood on the corner.

Cars automatically hit the brakes as they approached the intersection.

"You're right," said Coleman. "They're actually slowing down."

"Told you," said Serge. "Every year there's newspaper stories of cops who dress up as holiday characters to catch speeders. So I figured since we already have the costumes, and these assholes drive way too fast in a neighborhood full of kids . . ."

"That doesn't look like a radar gun."

"It's not," said Serge, aiming at another car that slammed the brakes. "It's just a black caulking gun from Home Depot."

"Wouldn't a hair dryer work better?" asked Coleman. "Why not use that instead of a caulking gun?"

"Because I don't want to look foolish."

Coleman watched another driver slam on the brakes. "You sure we won't get in trouble doing this?"

"There's no law against standing on a street corner dressed like an elf and pointing caulking guns at traffic. That's the whole problem with the general population: They're blind to the obvious possibilities."

"But isn't it against the law to impersonate police officers?"

"I'd say the elf suits are a good defense that we're making a strong effort not to look like cops."

"But you said they dress up like holiday characters to catch speeders."

"That's right." Serge aimed the caulking gun at an approaching car. "It's the police who are impersonating elves. We're the ones who should have the beef."

Crash!

"Serge." Coleman pointed at steam shooting out from under a hood. "That guy hit the brakes when he saw your caulking gun, and the other guy rear-ended him."

The drivers were out of their cars, cursing each other in the street. Just about to come to blows.

"Everybody just calm down!" yelled Serge, running into the road. "You were speeding, and you were following too close. But since it's so close to Christmas, I'm going to let you off with a warning." He began walking away.

One of the motorists: "Thank you, officer."

"Oh, I'm not a police officer," said Serge. "Just a concerned elf with a caulking gun. Please drive safely."

They went back to the house.

An hour later, electrical cords crisscrossed the lawn.

Serge stood at the top of a ladder, one step above where the warning label said not to step above. "Coleman, hand me another string of lights."

"I'm tired."

"Just hand 'em!"

Coleman grudgingly complied, reaching into an enormous box at his feet. "You bought twenty cases of lights. It filled the whole car and trunk, and I had to sit with the last box in my lap."

"This is going to be the best display in the whole city! . . . Give me another string."

Coleman handed it up. "But why do we have to go through all this work if we're just going to take it all down in a couple weeks?"

"Because that's the true meaning of Christmas. Running up the December electric bill." Serge draped another strand over a palm frond.

"How much more do we have to do?"

"Almost finished." Serge jumped down from the ladder. "We covered all the shrubs, and the roof, and palm trees, and garbage cans, and the pile of yard waste, and the broken washing machine we rolled down to the curb. And just in time because it's starting to get dark. I can't wait to turn it all on and win total respect from the street."

"What about that giant display on the next block with the inflatable snowman and life-size reindeer?"

"That guy's obsessive. The street will just think he's weird like the people who fill their yards with birdbaths and Roman statuary."

"Serge, the sun's almost down and you have four cases left. I don't think we're going to make it."

"I will if you don't slow me down." Serge tore open a cardboard flap. "Here, take some lights from this case and make your own decoration."

"Where?"

"The blank spot on the wall next to the front windows. Use this special tape."

Serge resumed with accelerated motion, frantically festooning case after case. Coleman slowly taped up a few strings of his own lights.

A half hour later, they finished at the same time. Serge beamed with pride. "There! Now, to set the whole neighborhood ablaze with good cheer!"

He grabbed the main power supply cable from the house, ready to plug it into the primary string of lights. "Countdown! Five, four, three, two, one—"

A screech of tires. A GTX with gold rims skidded up to the curb in front of the Davenport residence.

Serge squinted and growled.

Inside the car, heavy necking.

"Wow," said Coleman. "They're really going at it."

"Mr. Snake is getting on my last nerve. Nicole is just a kid."

"They're going at it even more."

Serge stepped forward for a better view. "That's too much activity for making out. Something's not right."

"Maybe they're doing it."

"Shut up, Coleman."

From the car: *"Stop! Let go of me! I said stop! . . ."*

"Look," said Coleman. "He's grabbing her wrists. Now she's screaming bloody murder."

"Motherfucker!" Serge was ready to blast into a sprint.

Coleman became puzzled. "Why are you stopping?"

"Over there." Serge pointed. "The front door opened. Jim's running down to the street. It will be better in Nicole's eyes if her father rescues her."

The screaming brought other neighbors out onto their porches, just in time to see Jim reach the car. He opened the passenger door and pulled Nicole free. They both tumbled backward onto the lawn.

The driver's door flew open. Snake raced around the car, tackling Jim. He jumped on top and began smashing away with pile-driver fists. Jim covered up the best he could, but still took an ugly beating to the face. Nicole jumped on Snake's back. "Get off my father!"

Snake turned and gave her a wicked backhand slap across the face, knocking the girl to the ground. Then returned his attention to Jim, pummeling away again.

Suddenly Jim felt Snake's deadweight collapse on him. He slowly uncovered his eyes to see Serge standing over them with brass knuckles on his right hand.

"Daddy!" Nicole crawled over, crying, and pushed Snake off him. "You're bleeding!"

"I'm okay, honey." Jim got up and hugged his daughter. Then he looked over at Serge. "Thank you."

Serge's mouth was solemn. "You two just go in the house."

Jim looked down. "But what about—"

"Don't worry about him," said Serge. "Forget all this happened. Right now you need to get inside and take care of each other."

Jim nodded, and he and Nicole walked toward the porch steps with arms around each other.

ONE HOUR LATER

A shuttle bus pulled up the driveway at Bayshore Manors.

The staff gingerly helped four elderly women out of the vehicle.

The facility's director came out in alarm. "Where'd you find them?"

"A club in Ybor City," said the driver. "With shirtless male bartenders."

"How'd they get the shuttle bus?"

A shrug.

"Okay, take them inside. It's getting late . . ."

The quartet of women shuffled into the dayroom to watch *Seinfeld* in syndication.

"They caught us," said Edna.

"So what?" said Edith. "They just brought us back. I told you we wouldn't get in trouble."

"They're going to do something," said Eunice.

"No they're not."

One of the caregivers walked over with a look of concern. "You really had us scared. Please don't do that again."

"Go fuck yourself."

The woman walked away.

Edith smiled at the others. "See?"

"Well, at least it was fun while it lasted," said Ethel.

"What are you talking about?" said Edith. "That just whetted my appetite."

"But they locked up the keys to the shuttle bus," said Eunice. "We won't be able to get away now."

"So we'll call a cab."

"And do what?" said Ethel.

"We need to hook up with someone we already know, for safe harbor." Edith got up and shuffled across the room. "So they won't be able to track us down next time."

"Where are you going?" asked Edna.

"To the computers."

"I don't think they'll let us on after what we pulled today," said Ethel.

"Of course they will," said Edith. "They're always encouraging us to get online and keep our minds sharp."

A few minutes later, the rest of the G-Unit huddled around Edith, tapping away on the keyboard.

"Facebook?" said Edna.

Tap, tap, tap. "You can find anybody on Facebook." A few more keystrokes. Edith sat back, gesturing at the screen. "And I just found him."

"*That* guy?" said Ethel.

Edith leaned forward again and typed. "I'll just send him a message, and then we wait and keep checking the computer until he responds."

"How do you know he'll respond?"

"I hit him with a snowball."

TRIGGERFISH LANE

Two hours after sunset. Four lawn chairs sat in a row on the front yard, facing the house.

A patio table at the end, with bottles of booze and an ashtray full of roaches.

"Hurry up already!" said City.

Country took a hit and stubbed out another joint. "Stupid Christmas lights. This better be good."

"It's going to be great!" said Serge. He held a pair of electric cords a few inches apart. "Countdown: three, two, one!" He plugged them in.

Their faces lit up with awe at the bright, reflected light of over a thousand colorful little bulbs.

"*Ooooooooooo.*"

Even City and Country were impressed.

"I especially like what you did with the palm trees," said City.

"Looks like a Corona beer ad," said Country. She turned back to the house. "But what's that dark spot. The lights didn't go on."

"That's Coleman's project."

"Serge," asked Coleman. "Can I do mine now?"

"Just one second," said Serge. "I want to set the mood. Did you know that the first Christmas ever celebrated in North America took place in the Sunshine State? It's true:

In 1539, the discoverer Hernando de Soto held festivities in Tallahassee, and since it's Florida, the spot is now marked by a kiosk." Serge looked up at the stars. "What must it have been like in such a pioneering time to experience Christmas in the yet-unexploited peninsula. Better still, what if de Soto had Christmas lights? These are the questions that need to be asked. What kind of decoration would such a courageous explorer create to commemorate the first Christmas in the New World? Let us pretend." Serge turned to his pal. "Go for it!"

Coleman held his own electrical cords. "Three, two, one!" He plugged them in. "Cool!"

The others stared curiously at the strands of Christmas lights forming an outline on the wall of a giant dick and balls.

"De Soto had unusual tastes," said Serge.

Across the street, Martha Davenport watched through the window with binoculars. The last set of lights caught her attention. "What the—?"

Serge stood up. "But we're not finished! My finest hour awaits!" He walked to the porch and returned with bigger wires and a control box like he was going to run a toy train set.

"What's that stuff?" asked Coleman.

"I got the idea from when I used to have a toy train set." Serge patted the control box. "I customized this from parts I bought at Radio Hut. The two big dials are variable voltage controls. I twist them back and forth to brighten and dim the lights."

"What for?"

"The crowning jewel of my kick-out-the-jams Christmas display! It's like building models as a kid. And what was the best part of building models?"

"That's easy," said Coleman. "Blowing them up with M-80s."

"Except I'm not going to blow something up. Actually sort of, but not really, but, well, you'll see."

Coleman reached in his pocket. "I definitely need to blow some gage for this."

"Mellow," said Serge. "We're on a neighborhood street. It's bad enough Country finished that last roach out here. We don't need to do anything strange to attract attention."

"I got the answer." Coleman snapped his fingers. "I'll use a one-hitter that looks like a cigarette."

"Regular brain trust out here."

Coleman packed the end of a thin metal tube painted white. "But those wires don't look like the others."

"Because they're not." Serge held one up for illustration. "My crown jewel needed more amperage, so I ran these special high-capacity extension cords from one of those weird outlets behind the oven in our kitchen. Then I spliced the control box to manipulate the effect. You know those crazy Christmas displays on YouTube where the lights dance to music?"

Coleman passed the hitter to Country. "There's going to be music?"

"No, but some serious audio. I was going to do this project anyway, but then a special feature fell into my lap . . ."

From the darkness: *You're a dead man! I am so going to kill you!*

Coleman turned to Serge. "I don't think Mr. Snake is enjoying this as much as we are."

"Because he doesn't have a personal involvement in the project like us. But that's about to change in a big way."

Serge reached for the left dial and ever so slowly turned it clockwise. Lights grew brighter.

The foursome raised their eyes. Snake sat in a chair at the very top of the roof, wrapped countless times with rope and Christmas lights . . . Getting brighter . . .

Coleman leaned over. "What's the second dial?"

"Volume control."

Coleman strained for a look at the roof. "I don't see any speakers."

"Snake is our speaker."

"But how . . . ?"

"You know all those piercings he has?"

"Like a pincushion."

"The other dial controls a second set of lights, except I removed the lights and wired their sockets to his piercings."

Coleman took a hit. "Righteous."

"Observe." Serge looked up and cupped his hands around his mouth. "Are you going to stay away from Nicole?"

"Fuck you! I'll do whatever I want!"

A quick twist of the dial.

"Ahhhhhh! . . . Dammit!"

"And I also want you to stay away from Jim and his whole family."

"Eat shit! . . . Ahhhhh! . . . Stop doing that!"

Serge winked at Coleman. "I think you get the picture."

"But, Serge," said Coleman, glancing up the street at people on porches. "Aren't you worried about the neighbors calling the police?"

"I have a strong feeling they're with me on this one. Everyone loves Christmas displays."

"So you're going to keep asking him questions like that until he agrees?"

Serge shook his head. "I'm not really interested in anything he has to say. Certain personality types tend to pull you into negativity. It's best not to dwell on them . . . Especially when we're out here to enjoy a special holiday moment."

"Rock on, dude!"

"The key is to twist the dials simultaneously, so the lights are in sync with the audio. I'll start with an easy one. Beethoven's Fifth Symphony."

Dials twisted four times.

"Ahh! Ahh! Ahh! . . . Ahhhhhhhh!"

"Sounds just like it," said Coleman.

And so Serge ran through a full program of songs.

"What was that last one?" asked Coleman.

" 'Flight of the Bumblebee.' " Serge pulled the control box close. "And now the grand finale. I'm just going to use the left dial, ever so slowly increasing the current to the lights. And because those lights aren't designed to stand the kind of power for an oven, they'll begin to explode individually, like popcorn in a microwave. The bulbs' filaments will burn out pretty quick, but also pretty hot."

"Will it electrocute him?"

"No, but he won't like it."

The dial began turning.

At first a few isolated pops spaced out seconds apart. Then, in rapid succession: *pop, pop, pop, pop, pop* . . .

It continued in a sadistic drumroll until the last light finally exploded.

From the roof: *"Okay, okay, you win! I'll never go near Nicole or her family again!"*

Neighbors on porches up and down Triggerfish Lane uniformly broke into applause.

Serge glanced at Coleman. "Like I said, total respect."

CHAPTER FIFTEEN

TWO DAYS BEFORE CHRISTMAS

An older-style Cadillac sat at the end of the Davenports' driveway.

Serge stared through binoculars.

"What's going on?" asked Coleman.

"Jim's mother is visiting for Christmas dinner."

"But it's not Christmas yet."

"I think there's some static between her and Martha." Serge watched her set the table with the best china. "Jim told me Martha goes off the stress meter whenever her mother-in-law visits."

"They fight?"

"Worse, this silent constant looming tension, Martha on the verge of a complete psychotic meltdown the whole time . . . So Jim told me they have his mom over just before Christmas, and then her parents just after. They reserve

Christmas Day itself for immediate family when their older children drive in from out of town."

Across the street, Rita Davenport entered the dining room to help Martha set the table.

"Mom, I really got this. Go talk with Jim and enjoy yourself."

"Don't be silly. I can't just stand around while you're doing all the work." Rita picked up a napkin, wiping down a fork Martha had already set beside a plate.

Martha's jaw clenched, blood pressure ticking upward. She faked a smile. "Excuse me a minute."

"Take your time." Rita wiped a spoon. "I've been doing this my whole life."

Martha marched into the kitchen. "Jim! She's wiping off the utensils I've already set."

Jim briefly covered his eyes with his hands. "Okay, I'll go talk to her."

"What are you going to say?"

"Just try to relax." Jim went into the dining room. "Mom, you don't need to do that."

"What? I'm not allowed to help?"

"I've got some new family photos I'd like to show you."

"Photos? Why didn't you say so? I must see." She followed Jim past the kitchen doorway and into the den, where framed photos stood atop an antique bureau.

Martha tiptoed down the hall to eavesdrop.

"Oh, Jim, these pictures are absolutely beautiful. The children have really grown."

"Yes they have, Mom."

"And I love how they're displayed on the bureau . . . Do you have a dust cloth and some Pledge?"

Martha's hands balled into white-knuckled fists . . .

Back across the street, Serge lowered the binoculars. "I feel so bad Martha and I have gotten off on about ten bad feet, because I really like Jim, and she's so terrific for him. But of course the reality of the situation is obvious: The absolute best thing I can do for both of them is never to go near their house for the rest of my life."

Coleman swayed with a bottle of rum and grabbed a chair for balance. "Huh?"

Serge stared at Coleman a moment. "I think you've got something." He began nodding. "There are no absolutes. I've locked myself into a defeatist mentality. Of course I can make it up to Martha! And because this is one of her most stressful days of the year with her mother-in-law, it's the perfect opportunity to help her out."

"But, Serge—"

He held up a hand. "Not now. When I was spying on them with the binoculars, they were just about to sit down to dinner, so I'll need to hurry." He headed toward the refrigerator. "I hear you're supposed to bring something . . ."

Back across the street, Jim carried the turkey into the dining room and set it on the table.

"Everything looks so delicious," said Rita.

They pulled out chairs and began sitting.

Ding-dong.

"Who can that be?"

Jim stood back up. "You two go ahead and sit. I'll answer it." He walked around the corner and opened the door.

"Jim!"

A gasp.

"I knew you'd look surprised. I've come to join you for dinner. I know it's last minute and all, but I hear it's okay if you bring something." Serge grinned and held up a crumpled brown paper bag. "I'm going to make it up to Martha, and then you'll be so proud of me. I'm going to be just like you someday!"

"Jim, who's at the door?" called Martha.

Serge slapped Jim on the shoulder—"Just leave everything to me"—and walked past him into the dining room.

"Surprise!"

Martha gasped.

"Who is this man?" asked Rita.

"I'm Serge Storms, super-close friend of Jim. And you must be his mom, who I've been hearing so much about." He walked up with an effervescent smile and kissed her hand. "You're even more radiant than I could have imagined."

"Serge," said Jim. "I don't think this is a good—"

Serge looked at the table. "I see I'm just in time."

"You're having dinner with us?" asked Rita.

Serge nodded and held up the crumpled bag. "I brought sides." He set the bag on the table and rummaged. "These are only a few days old—five tops." He began pulling out Kentucky Fried Chicken containers. "Here's coleslaw to die for, and the mac and cheese that Coleman barely touched, and a few biscuits. Heads-up, they're a little hard . . ."

Nicole covered her mouth and giggled.

Martha shot Jim a tense glance.

"Serge," said Jim. "I think there's been a misunderstanding. This is my mother's special day with us. It's always just family."

"Nonsense," said Rita. "He's a good friend of yours, and I must say very well mannered."

"But, Mom," said Martha.

"We've got more than enough food," said Rita. Then turning to Serge: "Why don't you pull up a chair and have a seat by me?"

Martha's temples throbbed.

Rita folded her hands on the table. "Jim, why don't you say the grace?"

"Mom, you know I'd really rather not—"

Serge's hand shot up in the air. "Oooo! Me! Me! Me! I'll say grace!"

Jim's and Martha's eyes bugged out.

"Why, Serge," said Rita. "That's extremely gracious of you. I'd love to hear you say grace."

"Okay, everyone, bow your heads." Serge closed his eyes and devoutly folded his hands. "Dear God, please ask your followers not to start any more wars."

Martha's head fell back over her chair.

Jim nearly fainted.

Nicole cracked up.

Rita Davenport slowly turned toward Serge. "That was a very interesting prayer. And a very good prayer. I know exactly what you mean: You're talking about the people in those *other* countries."

"Well, what I actually meant was—"

Jim's hand shot out and grabbed Serge's arm. "Leave it."

Serge shrugged.

Dinner and conversation proceeded with the tension of a midnight execution.

At the end, Rita set down her fork. "I'll be dead soon."

"That's an excellent philosophy," said Serge. "Don't take a single day for granted. Live life to the fullest!"

"No," said Rita. "I'm talking about getting old. I'm worried what will happen to me."

"What's to worry about?" said Serge. "You can always move in here. I'm sure they'd love to have you."

Martha spit out her food.

"Serge," said Jim. "We don't have enough room."

"What are you talking about?" Serge spread his arms. "You've got plenty of room. I know the layout of the whole place, especially upstairs, except that's a touchy subject. The point is, it's a golden chance for all of you to spend a lot more time together."

Martha began shaking, and grabbed a fork like a weapon.

Rita set her napkin on her plate. "I need to powder my nose. Jim, where do you keep the bleach?"

Serge's head snapped back. "Back up. Did you say 'bleach'?"

"Yes?"

"*Bleach*," said Serge. "Is that supposed to be some kind of joke?"

"No, is there something wrong with that?"

"Not if you're cleaning needles to shoot heroin, but otherwise, yes."

"I'm not sure I understand," said Rita.

"Jim," said Serge. "I just ran the floor plan through my head, and you're right. There isn't enough room after all."

Rita looked perplexed. "But I thought you said a minute ago they had a lot of space."

"Oh, there's plenty of room, just not for you."

"Did I say something wrong?" asked Rita.

"'Bleach,'" said Serge. "There's a lot I don't know about women, but I was married briefly, and I know about 'bleach.'"

"I didn't mean anything by it."

"You're talking to someone who practically invented mind games." Serge stood and sneered. "Martha invited you into her home, and Jim is your loving son. And you come in here with so-called idle comments, which disrespect Martha, put Jim in an awkward spot, and insult their marriage. And somehow you enjoy deliberately fanning this unpleasantness."

"Well!" said Rita. "If I'm not welcome here!"

"Don't stay on my account," said Serge. "I'll even kick-start your broom."

"Oh! I never!" Rita grabbed her purse and stormed out the door.

Serge turned back to face the stunned expressions around the table. "Oh my gosh, what have I done?" He lowered his head. "You must think I'm horrible. I can't stop screwing up when it comes to your family. So I'm going to leave now, and I promise you'll never see me again."

He started for the door.

"No," said Martha. "Come back and have a seat. Would you like some dessert?"

CHAPTER SIXTEEN

CHRISTMAS EVE

A '72 Chevelle whipped up the driveway.

Coleman pulled something out of a bag. "It's called a Yule log."

"Put that away," said Serge. "It's disgusting."

"Women dig it." Coleman slid a switch. A humming sound. "Got three speeds. And a Christmas theme. Here are little reindeer along the side, and Santa's cap on the end."

They got out of the car and headed for the house. "But why would you think a vibrator would be an appropriate gift for Martha?"

"You said Jim asked you for help with a present."

"Just put it back in the bag before the neighbors see that horrible thing . . . Wait, what's that music coming from the house?"

"Early Jackson 5," said Coleman. " 'Dancin' Machine.' "

"I know the song. It just sounds extra loud, and the girls usually aren't up this early." He stopped at the Christmas tree stuck in the doorway.

"What's that hanging from one of the branches?" asked Coleman.

Serge held the satin in his hand. "First-place ribbon from the neighborhood committee."

They got on hands and knees, and crawled into the house.

Serge slowly stood. "What the hell?"

City and Country were dancing up a storm.

"Yo, Serge," said Country. "Your friends are a hoot."

City spun a shorter person, busting a tango move. "Never would have guessed you knew normal people."

Coleman nudged Serge in the ribs. "I think it's the G-Unit."

"I know who they are . . . Hey, Edith, what on earth are you doing here?"

Edith moved her arms up and down to the lyrics, performing the robot. "Just gettin' my swerve on."

"I sensed that vibe." Serge set his McMuffin breakfast on the table. "But how did you find me? I'm off the grid . . . If you could, then the cops . . ."

"Take a chill pill," said Country. "We get the credit."

"What are you talking about?"

"I went to check our Facebook page, except you were signed in, so we decided to take a peek at your circle of friends and found their message . . ."

". . . Figured why not invite 'em over?" said City. "At

least it would break this stupid boring routine of you obsessing about Christmas." She casually lifted a foot as a model train ran underneath. "Turned out they're a blast."

"What's that?" asked Edna.

"What's what?" asked Coleman, wadding up a shopping bag.

"That thing you stuck on the shelf."

"It's called a Yule log. It's a—"

"I know what it is," said Edna. "Let me have it."

Coleman tossed, and Edna caught it on the fly.

Edith reached. "I want to see it."

Edna pulled away. "I spotted it first."

Serge suddenly jumped.

"What's the matter?" asked Coleman.

"Someone just goosed me." Serge turned and wagged a finger at Eunice, who giggled and ran away.

Coleman elbowed Serge again. "Old times."

No response.

"Serge? . . . Serge, what is it?"

Serge was concentrating on the view out the window. "There's that Ford Focus station wagon again."

"What's it doing?"

"Slowing down outside the Davenport place. Now it's speeding away, just like the Dodge Ram that won't be coming by anymore. And the black Delta 88 I saw again this morning."

"Probably a coincidence." Coleman raised tequila to his lips. "Let's do something. It's Christmas Eve."

Serge snapped his fingers. "You're right! It is Christmas

Eve. We're *required* to do something, and I know exactly what that is." He turned to a roomful of dancing. "Yo! G-Unit! . . ."

" . . . *Stayin' alive! Stayin' alive, ooo, ooo, ooo, ooo . . . Stayin' aliiiiiiiiiive . . .*"

"Serge, the music's too loud."

Serge made a shrill wolf whistle with two fingers in his mouth. "May I have your attention, please!"

"Still too loud."

Serge reached for the volume knob on the stereo.

" . . . *Stayin' alive—*"

Silence.

"Hey!" said Edith. "That's our theme song."

"I have an important announcement to make." Serge clapped his hands sharply for emphasis. "How'd you girls like to have some fun?"

"We're down with fun," said Edna. "Count us in!"

"Better hear what it is first," said City. "Never know with these guys."

"It's going to be great!" said Serge. "We'll all go caroling!"

Non-enthusiastic stares.

"What's the deal?" said Serge. "Everyone goes caroling."

"Sounds like we'll take a pass," said Country.

"I can't allow it," said Serge. "Besides, you're thinking of regular caroling. That's what everyone does. We're going Xtreme Caroling . . . I'm taking Christmas big!"

"What's Xtreme Caroling?" asked Eunice.

Serge looked over his shoulder. "Coleman, get the boom box . . . Okay, ladies, here's what we do . . ." And he laid it all out. When he was finished: "What do you think?"

"I'm in," said Ethel.

"Me, too," said Edith.

"But what do we wear?" asked Eunice, gesturing at the G-Unit's matching apparel. "We can't go around the streets in our nightgowns and slippers."

"Already thought of that," said Serge. "I know exactly what you need to wear."

"What?"

"I'd like to surprise you." He grabbed his car keys. "Come on, Coleman, supply run! . . . The rest of you start getting ready—and keep practicing what I showed you. It'll be dark soon . . ."

JUST AFTER DARK

A '72 Chevelle skidded back up the driveway.

Serge scrambled under the Christmas tree in the doorway. He stood and raised a shopping bag in each hand. "You're going to love it!"

The G-Unit grabbed the sacks and pulled out the purchases. "We're supposed to wear this?" said Edith.

"It'll be a gas," said Edna. "Let's put them on."

Fifteen minutes later, they were all ready.

Serge fit a green felt hat onto his head, and waved an arm forward like an infantry commander. "Follow me!"

Under the Christmas tree they went.

The unlikely alliance of eight people walked single file up Triggerfish Lane.

"When do we get going?" asked Edna.

"We'll start at the end of the block," said Serge. "Then work our way back down."

They reached the last house.

Serge walked up the porch steps of a pastel-peach 1929 bungalow. A finger pressed a button.

Ding-dong.

Inside: *"Honey, are you expecting anyone?"*

"No."

The door opened.

"Hello—" The woman's smile disappeared. Her expression didn't become one of alarm as much as: Improper Data Input. ". . . Uh, can I help you?"

"We're carolers!" said Serge. "More specifically, Xtreme Carolers."

"I've never heard of Xtreme Carolers," said the woman.

"Nobody has, until now!" Serge turned to Coleman. "Hit it!"

Coleman reached for a switch on the boom box . . .

A minute later, the woman called into the house: "Honey, come quick. You have to see this."

Her husband trotted down the hall. "What is it?"

"Just look."

Out on the lawn, a boom box thumped at top volume, heavy on the bass. Kool & the Gang's "Jungle Boogie." Except the carolers had modified the words.

The G-Unit stood in a line, each wearing a tiny green elf

suit. In unison they thrust their hips and pumped their fists by their sides, first to the left, then to the right.

Edna and Edith: *". . . Christmas boogie! Da-da-da, Da-da-da! Christmas boogie! Da-da-da, Da-da-da! . . ."*

Eunice and Ethel: *". . . Get down, get down! . . . Get down, get down! . . ."*

Behind them, Coleman ran weaving and stumbling with a lit pair of sparklers in his hands. Coming the other way, Serge did a string of cartwheels the length of the yard. City and Country stood on the sidewalk, rolling their eyes and shaking their heads.

". . . Christmas boogie! . . ."

Edith: *"Shake it around!"*

". . . Christmas boogie! . . ."

Edna: *"With the funk, y'all!"*

The song ended with a bow from the entertainers.

The couple on the porch applauded heartily. "Bravo!"

"Wait here," said the woman, heading back into the house. "I want to get you something . . ."

House after house, same reaction. More applause. "They're so cute . . ."

And on down the street. Coleman caught up with Serge on the sidewalk. "This is excellent. Everyone's forcing eggnog on us." He guzzled from a to-go cup. "I didn't know people would just give you liquor if you knocked on their doors and did shit in their yards . . . Caroling rules!"

"You need to be more careful with those sparklers. At the last house you singed your hair."

"I don't mind." He raised his cup to the sky. "Free booze!"

Serge grabbed his arm.

"Hey, man, it's cool," said Coleman. "Nobody's going to pinch us for open containers on this street."

"It's not that." Serge stopped and watched red taillights slow down a half block away. "There's that Delta 88 again, driving by Jim's house."

"Probably a real estate agent."

"I got this feeling," said Serge. "Just keep your eyes open."

More houses and applause, until they finally arrived at 888 Triggerfish Lane.

"Martha," said Jim. "Come out here and see this."

"... *Get down, get down!* ..."

"Ahhh!" Coleman pulled off his burning elf hat and stomped on it.

Serge pressed another button on the boom box.

"... *It's getting hot in here, so take off all your clothes* ..."

Clapping from the porch at the conclusion.

"Why doesn't everybody come inside and join us?" said Jim.

"Yes," said Martha. "Come on in. We have eggnog."

Coleman almost knocked everyone over running up the steps.

Serge yelled after him: "Wipe your feet!"

Coleman hit the brakes and shuffled elf shoes on the welcome mat.

Soon they were all seated around the living room on sofas and lounge chairs. Small talk. Martha made the rounds, pouring eggnog in clear coffee cups.

"Can I pick what's on TV?" asked Serge, changing channels before getting an answer. "The Grinch is stealing Christmas."

Coleman found something in his pocket. "I brought you an ornament." He hung a candy-cane shiv on their tree.

Everyone smiled at one another in the warm hearth of holiday neighborliness.

"It's been a long time," Jim told the G-Unit. "Where are you living now?"

"We're on the run," said Edith.

"They had us living in this rest home with condescending caregivers and afternoon pudding," added Edna. "But we said bullshit on that."

Serge elbowed Coleman. "What's wrong with you?"

Coleman looked wide-eyed, up and down the Davenports' Christmas tree. "What do you mean?"

"You're acting weird," Serge snapped in a loud whisper.

"The little lights," Coleman said, entranced. "They're like fireflies swirling around the tree, playing tiny harps."

"Did you take something again?"

"Oh no, absolutely not," said Coleman. "No, no, no. Yes, actually a lot."

"What did you take?"

"Mistletoe."

Serge blinked hard. "Mistletoe?"

Coleman nodded, snatching at the air with his hand for a nonexistent glow bug. "Mistletoe gets you high."

"But mistletoe's poisonous," said Serge. "*Extremely* poisonous. Severe gastrointestinal toxin, and a potentially life-threatening drop in pulse. The hallucinations are just a side effect."

"Fair trade-off." Coleman snatched the air again. "Cool."

Serge grabbed his wrist. "We have to get that crap out of your stomach."

"Uh-oh." Coleman put a hand on his tummy. "Think I'm going to be sick."

"Don't you dare throw up on the sofa." Serge pointed sideways with a thumb. "Martha just started liking us. Even if it's just a small amount of puke, women get funny about it."

Coleman's head began to loll. "Ooooo, definitely going to be sick."

"That's the two-minute warning," said Serge. "To the bathroom, now!"

Serge propped Coleman up and began leading him with an arm around his waist.

"Is everything okay?" Martha asked with concern.

"Just something he ate," said Serge.

"Fireflies," said Coleman, snatching air and opening an empty hand in disappointment.

Serge grinned nervously at Martha. "Where's your bathroom? Preferably one of the less nice."

Martha turned and pointed. "Just down the hall on the left."

"Thanks." Serge gave Coleman a tug around the waist. "Come on, you!"

Jim walked over to his wife. "Is everything all right?"

"Something Coleman ate . . ."

Outside, a vehicle with its lights off turned the corner

of Triggerfish Lane and rolled slowly down the street. At the other end of the block, another car came around the corner and also killed its lights. The first vehicle, a Ford Focus, slowed and parked at the curb three houses east of the Davenport residence. The other, a black Delta 88, parked three houses west.

Drivers' doors opened simultaneously. Two silhouettes ambled toward each other on the sidewalk. But their attention was elsewhere, eyes trained on the Davenports' brightly lit porch.

Inside, Martha smiled warmly at City and Country. "So where do you know Serge from?"

"Saint Pete. We all had warrants at the time."

Martha maintained composure and decided to change the topic. "Edith? How's life been treating you?"

"Like a bitch on roller skates." She handed Martha a small, gift-wrapped package with a big red bow.

"What's this?"

"It's your present. Serge was helping Jim pick something out for you."

Martha unwrapped it and stared.

"It's called a Yule log," said Edna. "Here's the power switch."

A humming sound.

"Trust me," said Country. "It'll rock your world like an earthquake. Especially if you put it in your—"

"Okay!" Jim sprang to his feet. "Anyone need more egg-nog? . . ."

Meanwhile, in one of the back bathrooms, Serge held

Coleman's elf hat and kept his head aimed for minimal mess and explanation. "There you go, big boy, get it all out."

"Oooo God, that feels better . . . Wait, some more . . ."

Back outside: Two silhouettes approached on the sidewalk, converging toward the Davenports' home. Fifty yards apart, the two men noticed each other, but in the dim light each considered the pedestrian coming toward him to be just a harmless night stroller out for fresh air. The first one slowed, so the second would pass before they got to the house.

The second one slowed, waiting for the other to pass.

Slower and slower until they both came to a complete halt on the sidewalk, twenty yards apart.

They squinted hard. Then their eyes flew open at the same time.

"You!" yelled the fired mall cop.

"You!" yelled the fired assistant mall manager.

They charged and tackled each other on the Davenports' lawn, rolling and clawing and pulling hair. Both reaching in vain for guns in ankle and belt holsters. A finger got bent back—*"Ahhhh!"*—an eye gouged—*"Ahhhh! . . ."*

Inside the house: "What's all that noise?" said Edith. "Sounds like someone's fighting."

"Seems to be coming from the yard," said Edna.

Jim walked toward the front. "I'll go check it out."

He opened the door. Shouting became louder. *"I'll kill you, motherfucker!"*

Martha headed for the door because she was concerned, and the G-Unit followed because they were nosy.

Two men scratched and punched, covered with grass and dirt. *"You're a dead man . . ."*

"I'll report you to the police!" yelled Martha.

They were too busy to listen. Then they rolled under better lighting.

"Jim," said Martha. "That looks like the mall cop I got fired. And the other one's the assistant mall manager I reported him to. I thought he had hair."

"He was bald when I fired him," said Jim.

"You fired the mall manager?"

Just then, the two men stopped rolling to catch their breath. They happened to look up at the couple standing on the front of the porch.

"You!" the ex-mall cop yelled at Martha and Jim.

"You!" the ex-manager yelled at Jim and Martha.

A spontaneous truce to unite against common foes. The men jumped up and charged the house, drawing their guns. Everyone scrambled inside and tried to close the door, but the security guard crashed through.

Soon everyone was crammed together on the largest sofa, silent, eyes following the two men pacing back and forth through the living room, cursing under their breaths and waving guns.

They crisscrossed again in front of the couch, each chugging from bottles of eggnog.

"I'm sure we can work this out," said Jim.

"Shut up!" The ex-manager spun with his pistol. "You fired me for nothing. And your stupid wife and her stupid anonymous report got me beat up!"

The guard stepped forward with his own gun. "You got me fired, and you hired professional elves to beat *me* up!"

"Maybe you should slow down on the drinking," said Jim. "In a situation like this—"

The guard and manager together: "Shut up! . . ."

Down the hall, Serge and Coleman crawled across ceramic tiles with big wads of toilet paper. "Make sure you wipe everything down and get every last speck. When it comes to bathrooms, wives are like those French boars that sniff out truffles."

Coleman pulled his head out from behind the toilet. "I think that's the last of it."

Serge fished through the cabinet under the sink. "Here's some air freshener."

He tossed it to Coleman, who sprayed liberally and set the can on the counter. "What do you think?"

"Smells like you threw up a bowl of potpourri."

"Did you hear something?" asked Coleman.

"Like what?"

"Yelling."

"Must be the TV." They left the bathroom and headed down the hall.

"There's the yelling again," said Coleman.

"Now that you mention it," said Serge. "I don't remember yelling in the Grinch special."

They came around the corner. The jingle bells gave them away. Curled felt feet slid to a stop on the hardwood floor. Two men aiming guns at them.

The security guard went ballistic with recognition. "You! You're the elves who attacked me in the restroom!"

"Wasn't us," said Serge. "Must have been those bad elves from the cheatin' side of town."

"Shut up!" Then a malicious smile. "The gang's all here. I get to take everyone out!"

"Hey," said the ex-manager. "I get some, too."

"Okay, we'll split," said the guard. "Plenty to go around." Then turning with rage again: "But the elves are mine! . . . Any last words before I blow your brains out?"

"Yes," said Serge. "I'd like to filibuster . . . The letter *A* is a vowel and the first in our alphabet derived from alpha in the Greek—"

"No filibuster!"

"The cloture rule isn't in effect," said Serge.

"Yes, it is!"

"I never heard a motion from the floor," said Serge. "Plus, you need a super-majority, and I'm pretty sure I've got the votes—"

"Shut up!"

"Parliamentary pussy."

"That's it! You die!" The guard stretched out his shooting arm.

From somewhere else: *"Now!"*

"What the—"

The ex-guard went down first. Then the former mall manager.

Horrible screaming. The two assailants desperately clawed the floor in an attempt to drag themselves to safety.

Four tiny elves swarmed like piranhas. Edith bit an ear, Edna an ankle. Ethel clubbed with the Yule log. Eunice pulled an ornament off the tree and stabbed.

The guard pulled a candy-cane shiv out of his neck. "We give up! Just get 'em off us! . . ."

Serge collected the dropped guns. "Okay, girls, you can get up now . . . Girls? . . . Girls!" He looked at Jim and Coleman. "I need a hand. They're in a frenzy. And keep your limbs away from their mouths."

The G-Unit was pulled off the home invaders, kicking and frothing.

"Nice work, gals," said Serge. "Now dial it down."

The quartet headed for the eggnog. "*That's* what I call fun!" said Edith.

Serge returned his attention to the two bleeding men. "What do you know? The home team rallies again." He handed Jim one of the guns, and motioned with the other toward the front door. "Might want to start drafting your own last words."

"Serge! No!" said Jim. "Don't do it!"

"Do what?" asked Serge. "We're just going to go out for some laughs . . ." He poked the gun barrel in their ribs. ". . . Right, fellas?"

"I can't let you do this!" said Jim.

"I'm impressed," said Serge. "You're actually confronting me. But they were after your family, and in your house."

"That's right," said Jim. "My family, my house, my rules . . . Besides, it's Christmas Eve. Look in your heart."

"I am," said Serge. "And I see your family's well-being.

If I don't take care of this and let you turn them over to the police, they'll eventually forget we showed them mercy. Then they get out of prison, where they've had time to do nothing but build a grudge. Some people tend to fixate."

"I have another idea," said Jim. "And you always claimed you wanted to be like me."

TV: *". . . Just then the Grinch's heart grew three times its normal size . . ."*

"True, true," said Serge. "Keep talking."

"They're angry at me because I fired them," said Jim. "But there's another part of my job because of the whole crazy, up-down stock market that dictates bad business decisions."

"What are you talking about?"

"Let me get my briefcase." Jim ran out of the room.

Serge smiled and shrugged at his prisoners.

Jim returned and opened the attaché case on a coffee table. "They gave me some work I'm supposed to hit after the holidays, but now's as good a time . . ." He pulled out a file folder. ". . . This is from my firm's contract with the mall. Seems they're a little short in the assistant manager position. And because of recent assaults in the restroom and manager's office, they're seeking someone with experience in the security industry." He looked up at the former guard. "What do you say?"

"Me? Assistant mall manager?" He lunged and hugged Jim. "Oh, thank you, thank you, thank you! . . ."

"Put me down now."

"Okay," said the guard. "You won't regret this."

"But what about me?" said the ex-manager.

"I'm getting to that," said Jim. He pulled out another file. "Because of those same assaults I just mentioned, the mall wants to beef up security. However, because of the anger management problems of recent hires, which resulted in unprofessional behavior toward customers, they're interested in at least some managerial experience . . . Want it?"

"Me? Mall cop?"

Jim nodded and braced himself for a hug that never came.

"Why not?" said the ex-manager. "I need the work, so sure, I'll take it."

The new assistant mall manager looked down and laughed at the new mall cop. "Imagine that! The guy who fired me, and now I'm his supervisor. Well, guess what? You're fired!"

"Hey!" the bald man said to Jim. "He can't do that, can he?"

"Yes, he can," said Jim, picking up a folder again. "But then that leaves me with a new opening. So you're hired."

"You're fired," said the new assistant manager.

"You're hired," said Jim.

"You're fire—"

Serge jumped in the middle. "Guys, guys! We can do this all night long . . . Now, are you two going to play nice together at the mall? Or do we have to go for a little ride?" Another gesture with the gun. "I've got plenty of room in the trunk."

The two new mall hires glanced at each other, then at Serge. "We'll get along."

"Great to hear it! . . . And, Jim, I'm even more in awe. You've taught me so much."

"I need to thank you, too," said Jim.

"Me, too," said Martha. She gave him a hug and peck on the cheek good-bye.

"G-Unit? City and Country?" said Serge. "Let's not wear out our welcome."

The women stood and tossed back the remains of their eggnog, then filed out the door.

"And, Jim," said Serge. "Better give me that other gun. You're not a firearms expert like me and don't know the rules of gun safety. A lot of people pick them up like this and—"

Bang.

Martha gasped. "My china cabinet! And favorite plates!"

"Guess that's my cue to leave . . . You need anything at all, we're just across the street."

"Serge," said Jim. "That gunshot. The police will be coming. I think you need to clear completely *off* the street."

"Don't be ridiculous . . ."

Sirens in the distance.

". . . On second thought." He stuck his head out the door. "Hey, gals, looks like a road trip's in the cards." Then he slapped Jim on the shoulder. "Merry Christmas, dude! . . . Merry Christmas, Nicole! . . . And, Martha . . . Martha? . . . Looks like she's overcome with emotion over my departure . . . Give her my best." Serge trotted out the door. "And try not to use that bathroom for a couple days . . ."

A '72 Chevelle was backed into its parking slot to hide the license plate.

Another anonymous run-down motel along the Gulf of Mexico in St. Pete Beach. But run-down in a positive way in Serge's book: un-updated, the original furniture and fixtures and god-awful period paneling, freezing the room in time, but clean. Relatively. And it really was anonymous, no sign, address number gone. Looked like it might be closed down, which was almost accurate. A few naked lightbulbs, the old-style orange ones, ran along the walkway by a single row of rooms. But to Serge, the biggest draw was the wild foliage, the canopy of sea grapes, birds of paradise, beach sunflowers, and anything else that not only required no maintenance, but would take over without it.

Serge had hit the brakes just after midnight. "This is it! I love Christmas in a depressing setting like a dumpy motel. Makes you appreciate it more."

Hours later.

Coleman snored with an alternating high-low-pitched whistle through a big booger.

"Wake up! Wake up!" said Serge. "It's Christmas!"

"Huh, wha . . . ? What time is it?"

"Five *A.M.*! It's been Christmas for hours! I wanted to wake you earlier, but I thought it might be too early, so I hung out with the night manager. You know what's funky? Little space heaters! I just love hanging out by one early Christmas morning with someone working alone on the overnight shift. Especially if they have whiskers and wine breath and seem like they want you not to bother them, which means they're lonely, so I offered to buy him Ripple from the convenience store across the street, but not before talking to the convenience store guy, because he also had a space heater, and almost forgot about the first guy until the cops came in for coffee and Slim Jims, so I ran back across the street with the Night Train, and the manager had fallen asleep, and I said, 'Wake up! Wake up! . . . It's been Christmas for hours!' and then he said 'fuck' a lot until I got the wine in him and he kicked his feet up and said his bones told him it was going to be a cold morning. And then I noticed the clock and remembered you, so here I am. Merry Christmas! And the old man was right: It's only forty-two degrees outside, overcast, and I'm flipping out!"

Coleman sat up on the side of the bed and smacked his cottonmouth lips together. "Why are you flipping out?"

"Since a white Christmas is out of the question, the best you can hope for in Florida is a non-sweaty Christmas. Let's open presents! Santa came! Santa came!"

Serge ran across the room and Coleman followed at a less enthusiastic pace. They took seats across from each other at a small table next to the window overlooking Gulf Boulevard. Clusters of predawn traffic raced by at intervals dictated by the traffic light up the street. In the middle of the table stood a pitiful little Christmas tree that Serge had bought overnight at a twenty-four-hour drugstore. Some of the lights blinked.

"What did I get! What did I get!" said Serge. He reached in a shopping bag, finding two cheerfully wrapped packages. "This one's for you, and this one's for me. Who goes first? Can I go first? Please?"

Coleman rubbed crust from his eyes. "Sure . . ."

Serge savagely ripped through the paper. "Oh my God, a vintage View-Master with a reel inside." He held it to his eyes and clicked through the 3-D photos. "It's the Overseas Highway from the forties! Here's how Sloppy Joe's looked almost seventy years ago!" He lowered the viewer. "Where'd you find it?"

"Antique store. You're always going on about those things."

Serge clapped his hands like a trained seal. "Open yours! Open yours!"

Coleman's present was round. He tore off the paper, then rotated the gift in his hand. "A coconut carved like a monkey's head. Cool." He began setting it down.

"But that's not all," said Serge.

Coleman looked at it some more. "I see now; it's a tropical drink cup. There's a hole on top for a straw."

"Getting warmer . . ." Serge said coyly.

Coleman scrunched his eyebrows and turned the coconut over again. "Wait, there's another hole in the back of the monkey's head, and a third in its mouth with a little bowl. It's not a cocktail cup at all; it's a bong! . . . But where'd you learn how to make one?"

"You helped me assemble it last night and then we wrapped it."

"I don't remember."

"Surprise!"

"I'll try it out right now." He packed the bowl.

"And I'll play with my View-Master. And then we'll watch the Charlie Brown special in the portable DVD player that I wired to the TV. Charlie Brown has a crappy Christmas tree just like ours. But if we stand around it and wave our arms, it becomes a great tree! . . . Coleman, stand up, join me! Let's wave our arms! . . . Why isn't it working?"

Several hours later.

A knock at the door.

Actually a foot kicking. Coleman answered. Serge rushed in with arms loaded down, followed by gusts of frigid air. Coleman closed the door quickly.

Serge set the bags on the table. "Christmas dinner's ready!" He shivered and rubbed his shoulders. "Man, the temperature's still dropping. The old dial thermometer they got nailed up outside the office says it's thirty-nine."

Serge and Coleman had rented room number three, which connected on either side to two other rooms, respectively occupied by the G-Unit and City and Country. They had all gathered in Serge's room, sitting on beds and awaiting his return with a promise of an ultra-traditional holiday meal.

"Here are the sides," Serge said as he emptied the bags. "And I got two buckets each of regular and extra crispy."

They dug in.

Coleman munched on a drumstick. "So what presents did you girls get?"

Edith bit into a crispy wing. "We all bought each other Yule logs."

Country licked her fingers and held up an envelope. "Serge got us gift cards for Hooters."

"That's a historic present," said Serge. "The very first one is just off the Courtney Campbell in Clearwater."

The afternoon wore on. Listless, overstuffed dinner casualties lay about the room digesting way too much food. Rum began to flow. Laughter filled the musty air as the eclectic group shared jokes and bonded. Serge continually darted in and out.

"Serge!" yelled City. "You're letting all the cold air in. Why do you keep running in and out?"

"Because the temperature's still dropping! The dial on the thermometer is down to thirty-three and still going south."

"What's that thing?"

Serge plugged an electric cord into the wall. A warm glow near the floor. "I bought a tiny space heater at the drugstore."

They all gathered round, holding out their palms.

Serge stood back in utter contentment. "This is the best Christmas ever! There's no possible way it can get any better!"

Country grinned mischievously. "Yes, it can get better."

"What are you talking about?"

She walked over. "You haven't seen your best gift yet." Then she planted a big wet one on him.

Serge glanced around with mild embarrassment. "You want to . . . now?"

"No, not *that*."

"Then what's this gift?" asked Serge.

The same devious smile again. Then she canted her head toward the window. "Look outside."

Serge did. His mouth fell wide as he walked stiffly across the room and placed his palms against the glass. Then he suddenly dashed out the door.

"Snow!"

The rest followed.

They were the tiniest of flakes that immediately melted in your hand, and there would be no accumulation, but it was indeed snow.

"What the hell is Serge doing now?" asked Edith.

"Running in circles in the parking lot," said Edna. "Catching snowflakes on his tongue."

The G-Unit silently looked at one another. Smiles broke out. They began running around the parking lot.

City glanced at Country. Two more smiles. They began running.

"Wait for me," said Coleman.

Serge stopped on the sidewalk to observe the parking lot full of people racing around and laughing themselves silly as they reverted to children, which was what it's all about. And Serge got a tear in his eye. "This is the best ever."

Then he turned to the street, spread his arms wide, and announced to mankind in general:

"I bring everyone great news of joy! The War on Christmas is over! So Merry Christmas, Happy Hanukkah, Happy Kwanzaa, and yes, for the co-existence crowd, Season's Greetings! . . . Catch you all next year!"

A NOTE ON THE TYPE

The text of this book was set in a face called Leubenhoek Gothic, the versatile eighteenth-century type developed by Baruch Leubenhoek (1671–1749), the Dutch master whose serif innovations last to this day. However, unsubstantiated accounts have recently surfaced that attribute Leubenhoek Gothic not to Baruch Leubenhoek, the stalwart traditionalist, but to the Hungarian Smilnik Verbleat (1684–1753?), the iconoclastic rebel of typography whose deconstruction of the alphabet into upper- and lowercase set the typesetting world aflame. It is indeed a compelling inquiry, since Leubenhoek Gothic is widely accepted as the most stunning example of the sturdy hot-face designs typified during the last golden age of typesetting, when the accomplished typemasters were nothing less than international celebrities. Stories abound of Leubenhoek unveiling a new typeface, setting fire to the neoclassical world, only to have Verbleat trump it later that week, triggering celebrations of Romanesque proportions. Such revelry often saw Leubenhoek and Verbleat become quite drunk and take nasty falls that would have sidelined men of lesser constitutions. And of course women were always available; Baruch was no slouch, but Smilnik's reputation for three-ways was unsurpassed. Soon new fonts appeared, each more daring. The reading world was ecstatic. Then, tragedy. In 1749, both were rumored to have been suffering from dementia associated with late-stage gonorrhea when they met up in Antwerp and pitched a heated argument about whether Smilnik's *s*'s really looked like *f*'s, and Verbleat crushed Leubenhoek's skull in with a clavichord.